W9-BRP-814

Cover illustrated by Art Mawhinney and Gil DiCicco
Illustrated by The Disney Storybook Artists

Bambi from the story by Felix Salten

Published by Louis Weber, C.E.O.
Publications International, Ltd.
7373 North Cicero Avenue
Lincolnwood, Illinois 60712

www.pilbooks.com

Manufactured in China.

8 7 6 5 4 3 2 1

ISBN: 0-7853-9739-6

Read to Me, Grandma

publications international, ltd.

Contents

Contents

Contents

To:
From:

Story adapted by Margot Boyer

Once upon a time there lived a princess named Snow White. She was a kind and loving girl, but her stepmother, the Queen, was jealous of her beauty. The Queen forced Snow White to do all the hardest work in the castle.

Each morning the Queen looked into her magic mirror and asked, "Magic Mirror on the wall, who is the fairest one of all?" Every morning the mirror answered, "You are the fairest." But one day, the mirror said, "Snow White is more beautiful than you." The Queen did not like this. She was determined to get rid of Snow White.

Outside, Snow White scrubbed the castle steps, singing as she worked. A handsome Prince riding near the castle heard her lovely voice. He climbed the castle wall and came near her as she stood by the well. When she looked down into the water she saw their faces reflected side by side. "Hello," smiled the Prince. Snow White knew that he was her true love.

The Queen heard the Prince talking to Snow White and grew angry. She called her faithful huntsman. "Take Snow White far into the forest to pick wildflowers and leave her there, far from any help," she ordered.

The Huntsman did not want to do this. "I could not hurt the little Princess," he stammered. But the Queen had no pity. The Huntsman was forced to obey her wishes.

The Huntsman led Snow White into the forest. She picked the beautiful blossoms and laughed at the wild birds in the trees. Suddenly, the Huntsman fell to his knees. "I'm sorry to frighten you, but you must know. The Queen wants to be rid of you. Go away into the forest and hide."

Snow White ran into the woods. It grew dark and the tree branches clutched at her dress. She stumbled into a pond. Her feet were wet and cold. Shining eyes stared at her from the darkness. She ran and ran. Exhausted, she lay on the ground and fell asleep.

At dawn, the forest awoke. Birds sang and small animals came out of their dens. They saw Snow White sleeping on the ground. They thought it was quite curious that a human would be deep in the forest like this.

A bunny sniffed at her. When Snow White felt the soft, warm nose on her hand, she lifted her head. All around her were adorable forest animals. They looked at her as if they were concerned.

"It was silly of me to be frightened," she said. The animals seemed to understand Snow White's every word. "I need a place to sleep," she said to the animals.

Excited, the animals led her through the woods. Soon they came to a pretty cottage beside a gentle stream. Snow White knocked on the door, but no one answered.

Snow White stepped inside. She saw a little kitchen with seven little chairs. Everything was dirty and covered with cobwebs. "It looks like messy children live here," Snow White said. Together, she and her forest friends cleaned the house. Snow White sang while they worked.

Upstairs, she found a bedroom with seven little beds. There was a name on each one. "Doc, Happy, Sneezy, Dopey, Grumpy, Bashful, and Sleepy," she read. Snow White lay down across the beds and fell asleep.

The cottage belonged to the Seven Dwarfs, who dug for jewels every day in their mine. The Dwarfs sang as they walked back to their cottage. They stopped suddenly when they saw the cottage lights on and the front door open. The Dwarfs were frightened as they snuck into their house.

"Who cleaned our cottage?" asked Doc.

"Maybe there's someone upstairs," Happy replied.

The Dwarfs went upstairs and found Snow White asleep. She woke up and smiled.

"Who are you?" asked Doc.

"I'm Snow White," she replied. "I need a place to stay."

The Dwarfs were glad to help. "Of course you can stay," they said.

Happily, they sat down to a nice dinner of stew, bread, and milk. After dinner they danced and sang together. At midnight, Snow White went upstairs to sleep, while the Seven Dwarfs lay down near the fire.

The wicked Queen learned that Snow White was living in the forest with the Dwarfs. She decided to get rid of Snow White once and for all. The Queen got out her books of magic spells and mixed a brew that turned her into an old woman with white hair. Then she mixed up a poison potion and dipped a red apple into it. She wrapped a black cloak around herself and headed into the forest.

When the Dwarfs left the cottage in the morning, Doc warned Snow White, "Beware of strangers." She promised to be careful and kissed each Dwarf good-bye as he went out the door.

Snow White was baking pies when a shadow fell across the window. An old peddler woman stood there. Snow White did not know that it was really the wicked Queen, but the birds knew. They flew at the old woman, trying to drive her away.

Snow White felt sorry for the old woman and invited her inside. The Queen took the red apple from her basket and gave it to Snow White. "This is a magic wishing apple," the Queen said. "Take one bite, and all your dreams will come true."

Snow White believed her. "I wish my Prince would carry me away to his castle," she said. Then she took a bite of the apple and fell to the floor.

"Now I'll be the fairest in the land," the old Queen cried with delight.

The birds and animals ran through the forest. They had to let the Seven Dwarfs know what had happened. They reached the mine just as the Seven Dwarfs got there. They pulled at the Dwarfs' clothes and beards in an effort to make them understand. "Something is wrong," said Doc. "Maybe something has happened to Snow White." Together, the Dwarfs and the forest creatures ran back to the cottage.

The Dwarfs reached the cottage and found Snow White lying very still. The apple remained in her hand. The Dwarfs were unable to awaken Snow White no matter how hard they tried. They were very sad. They built a special bed of gold and crystal and laid Snow White upon it in a beautiful forest glade surrounded by flowers.

Autumn came and went, as did winter. Finally, spring arrived. One day, the Prince came riding by on his white horse, singing a sad, sweet song. He had searched far and wide for his true love. As he came into the glade, the sun shone on Snow White's face.

The Prince gazed at Snow White's beauty. He knelt down on one knee and gently kissed her red lips.

Snow White sighed and stretched as if she were just waking up from a nap. She opened her eyes and saw the Prince standing before her. They opened their arms and drew each other into an embrace.

The Dwarfs were filled with joy. They sang and laughed and danced in circles in the meadow. The birds sang with happiness, and the forest animals chirped and capered and scampered. Love's first kiss had awakened the sleeping Snow White.

Tenderly, Snow White said good-bye to the Dwarfs and to all the forest creatures. The Prince lifted Snow White onto his white horse. Together they rode off into the golden light of the setting sun.

TOY STORY

Story adapted by Lisa Harkrader

Woody, the cowboy doll, was worried. Today was Andy's birthday and Woody had been Andy's favorite toy for a long time. Woody was worried that Andy might get a new toy that he would like better. Plus, Andy and his family were moving to a new house tomorrow. What if Andy left Woody behind?

Andy's friends arrived at the party. They all carried brightly wrapped gifts. Woody and the other toys couldn't go downstairs to the party, so they used the baby monitor as a walkie-talkie. Woody was able to hear Andy as he opened his gifts.

Andy opened a board game.

"Whew!" said Woody. "Andy won't like a board game better than his old toys."

Andy opened a lunch box and a set of bed sheets.

"Whew!" said Woody. "He won't like those things better than us."

Then Andy's mom brought out a special surprise gift. Woody listened as Andy opened it.

"Cool!" said Andy. "Thanks, Mom!"

Woody didn't know what the gift was. But he knew Andy loved it.

Andy ran upstairs to put his new toys away. He placed his surprise gift in Woody's place on the bed. Then Andy and his friends ran outside to play.

Woody climbed up onto Andy's bed to see the surprise gift.

"Greetings," said the new toy. "I am Buzz Lightyear of Star Command. I come in peace."

"You're Andy's new toy?" said Woody.

"No, I'm a space ranger," said Buzz.

"You're a toy," said Woody.

"I'm a space ranger," said Buzz. "And I can prove it. I can fly." Buzz pushed a button on his space ranger suit. Two wings popped out. "To infinity and beyond!" he cried.

Buzz leaped into the air. His wings caught on the mobile hanging from the ceiling. Then he fell to the floor, landed on a rubber ball, and bounced back onto Andy's bed.

"See?" said Buzz proudly.

"That wasn't flying," Woody grumbled. "That was falling with style."

But Andy loved Buzz. The other toys liked Buzz, too. They were mad at Woody. They thought Woody wanted to get rid of Buzz.

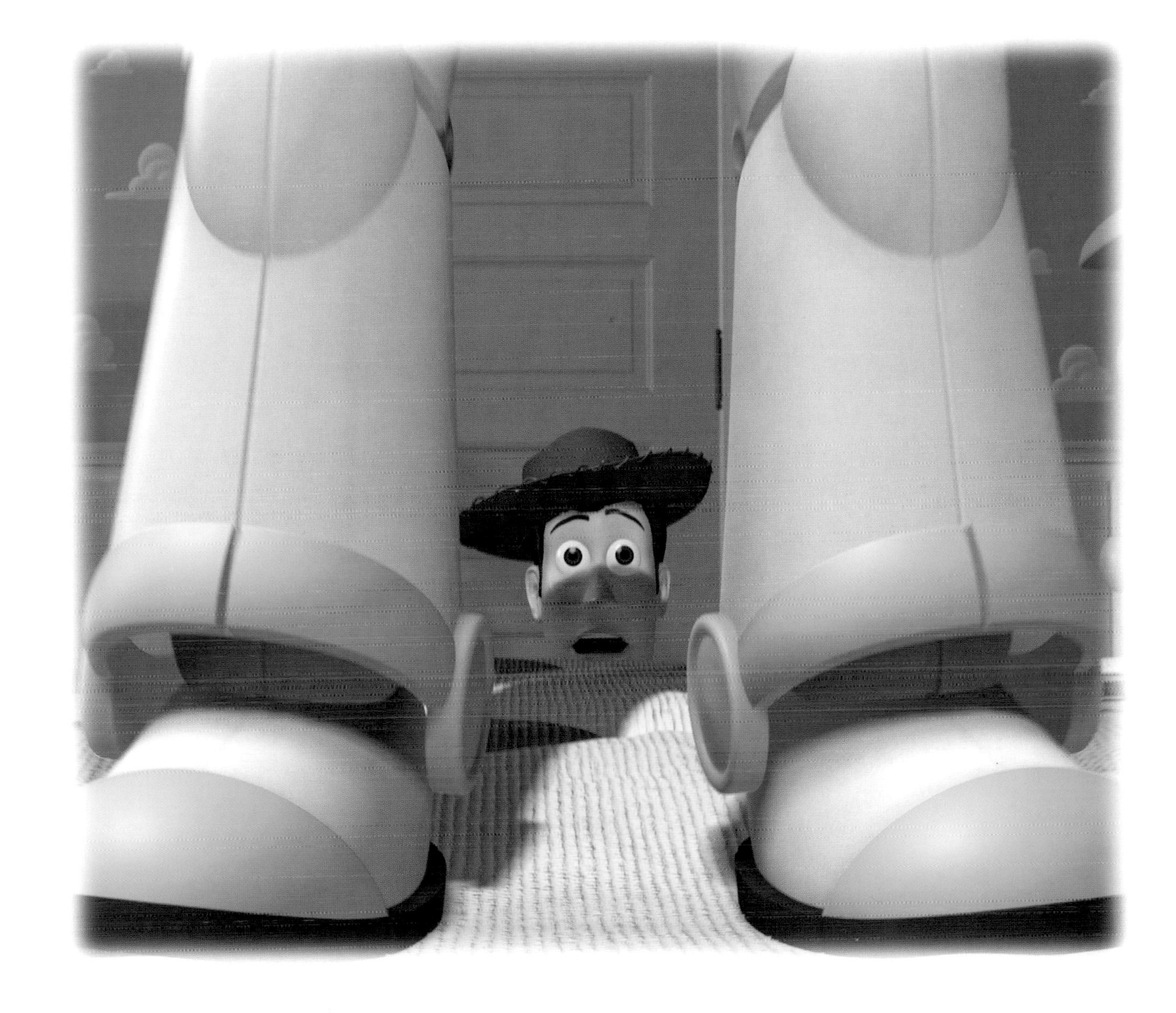

The next afternoon, Andy's family went to Pizza Planet for lunch. Andy took Woody and Buzz along. Pizza Planet was filled with games. Buzz began looking for a spaceship.

"I must return to my home planet," he said.

Woody shook his head. "You don't have a home planet. You're a toy."

"No, I'm a space ranger," said Buzz. "Out of my way, Sheriff."

Buzz strode across Pizza Planet toward one of the games. It was shaped like a rocket ship. Buzz climbed inside.

"Oh, no!" said Woody. "That's the claw game. Somebody will pick up Buzz with the claw and take him home. Andy will never see him again. The other toys will think I lost Buzz on purpose."

So Woody climbed into the claw game, too. But before he could get Buzz out, a boy put a quarter into the game. Woody looked and saw the boy.

"It's Sid!" said Woody.

Sid lived next door to Andy. Sid was mean to his toys. He poked nails in them. He blew them up with firecrackers.

Sid lowered the claw. It closed around Buzz. Woody grabbed onto Buzz's feet and tried to pull Buzz from the claw. But Sid saw Woody first.

"Cool!" said Sid. "Double prizes."

Sid put Woody and Buzz in his backpack and took them home to his bedroom. Woody was nervous.

Woody and Buzz waited until Sid left, and then they crept from the backpack. Sid's toys came out of hiding at the same time. Sid's toys were scary-looking. Sid had pulled their arms, legs, and heads off and put them on the wrong bodies. They were scary enough to make Woody and Buzz run from the room.

But they didn't get far. Sid's vicious dog, Scud, barked and chased them down the hall. Woody hid in a closet. Buzz escaped into the family room. The TV was blaring. Buzz saw a commercial for a Buzz Lightyear action figure.

"Action figure?" said Buzz. "Was Woody right? Am I really a toy? I know how to find out."

"To infinity and beyond!" he cried as he leaped toward an open window. But instead of flying, Buzz fell to the floor. His arm popped off.

Sid's sister, Hannah, saw Buzz, took him to her room, and dressed him in doll clothes. When Woody found Buzz, he was having a tea party with Hannah's dolls.

SPACE RANGER
LIGHTYEAR

"Come on, Buzz," said Woody. "We've got to get out of here."

"I can't help you, Woody," said Buzz. "You were right. I'm not a space ranger. I'm just a toy. I couldn't even fly out the window."

"The window?" said Woody. "Buzz, you're a genius. We'll escape out the window in Sid's room."

Woody dragged Buzz back to Sid's room. Before they could climb to the window, Sid's toys slithered out from hiding again and surrounded Buzz.

"Leave him alone!" said Woody.

The toys grabbed Buzz and his broken arm.

"Don't hurt him," said Woody. "He's my friend."

When they finally let Buzz go, he was fine. He was better than fine. His broken arm was back in place.

Woody stared at them. "You fixed him," he said. "Why, you're not scary at all. You're nice."

At that moment, the door burst open and Sid rushed in. He was carrying a box.

"It came!" said Sid. "My rocket finally came. Now, what should I use it on?" He glanced down and saw Buzz. "I've always wanted to send a space man into space."

He strapped the rocket onto Buzz's back and took him outside.

WAR
KEEP OUT OF RE
LASER

Woody and the rest of the toys raced downstairs. They slid through the dog door to the backyard. They saw Buzz on a platform that Sid had built. Sid was just about to light the rocket. Woody acted quickly.

"Put your hands in the air," called Woody.

"What?" Sid looked around. He saw Woody. "Oh, it's just that wimpy cowboy doll." He picked up Woody.

"We're tired of the way you treat your toys," said Woody. "We want you to stop torturing them. We'll be watching you, Sid, so play nice."

The other toys rolled toward Sid, who screamed and dropped Woody. "They're alive!" he cried. "The toys are alive!" He ran into the house.

Buzz leaped from the platform. "Woody, look," said Buzz. "I hope we're not too late."

Buzz pointed next door toward Andy's house. The movers had finished loading the family's things into their truck. They were ready to leave. Andy's family was about to leave in their van, too.

Woody and Buzz raced toward Andy's house. But when they got there, the van and the truck had already pulled out of the driveway.

Woody and Buzz ran after the moving truck. They were just barely able to catch up to it and climb aboard. But Sid's dog, Scud, chased after them. He grabbed Buzz's leg and pulled him from the truck.

"I'll save you!" called Woody.

Inside the truck, Woody found Andy's remote control car, RC, in one of the boxes. He jumped on RC and raced back down the street. Woody rescued Buzz, but RC's batteries died before they could return to the truck.

"Don't worry," said Buzz. "I've got a rocket."

Woody lit the rocket strapped to Buzz's back. Buzz grabbed Woody, and Woody grabbed RC. They shot down the street. RC landed in the back of the truck, but Woody and Buzz flew right over it. Buzz popped his wings out, and the rocket broke free. Woody and Buzz soared through the air.

"Buzz, you're flying!" said Woody.

"No," said Buzz. "I'm falling with style."

Woody and Buzz dropped through the sunroof of Andy's van. They landed in the box next to Andy.

"Mom!" cried Andy. "It's Woody and Buzz! They're here in the car."

Andy hugged Woody and Buzz all the way to his new house. They were both his favorite toys.

Sleeping Beauty

Story adapted by Lynne Roberts

In a faraway land, long ago, there lived a king and queen. They were very kind people and ran their kingdom with love and compassion. They loved each other very much and wanted a child with whom to share their love. One day, their wish came true. The Queen gave birth to a beautiful baby girl. The birth of the Princess filled their lives with so much sunshine, they decided to name the girl Aurora, which means "dawn."

King Stefan and his Queen declared Princess Aurora's birthday a holiday. Everyone in the kingdom was invited to a splendid party to welcome the new baby. Guests came from all over the kingdom, from nearby lands, and from faraway places. The most welcome guests were the three good fairies, Flora, Fauna, and Merryweather. Not invited to the party, however, was the evil fairy, Maleficent.

At the party, King Stefan promised King Hubert that Aurora would marry Hubert's son, Prince Phillip. This would ensure that both children would marry royalty and that the two kingdoms would be safe.

When it was time for presents, the three fairies wanted to give baby Aurora very special gifts. Each would take a turn casting her magic spell. Flora gave Aurora the gift of beauty. Fauna gave Aurora the gift of song. But just as Merryweather was about to give Aurora her gift, Maleficent burst into the room.

Maleficent was very angry that she had not been invited to the party. She knew that people did not like her. She wanted to ruin the birthday party for Princess Aurora and make everyone in the kingdom unhappy. She decided to cast an evil spell on the baby.

"Before sundown on her sixteenth birthday," said Maleficent, "the princess will prick her finger on the spindle of a spinning wheel and die!" She knew that for the next sixteen years, the kingdom would live in fear. After her spell was cast, the evil fairy left. King Stefan and the Queen were terrified for their daughter. They couldn't bear the thought of anything bad happening to her.

Flora, Fauna, and Merryweather told King Stefan and the Queen not to worry. Merryweather still had her gift to give to Aurora, and although she could not reverse the evil spell, she could make it better. Merryweather thought and thought. Finally, she said that when Aurora pricked her finger, she would not die, but rather, would fall into a deep sleep.

"Aurora will awaken," said Merryweather, "with a tender kiss from her true love."

To be safe, King Stefan ordered that every spinning wheel in the entire kingdom be burned. He did not want to take any chances that Aurora would prick her finger on a spindle. Every single spinning wheel that could be found was burned that day.

The people of the kingdom still feared that something terrible would happen to Aurora as she grew up. The fairies had an idea. They told King Stefan and the Queen that they would hide Princess Aurora deep in the forest until her sixteenth birthday. They would raise the girl as their own. The three fairies would pretend to be peasant women and would not use their magic. They felt that using magic would attract too much attention and Maleficent would surely find them.

The King and Queen agreed to this plan. They knew that they would miss their baby girl very much, but they also knew that this was the only way to keep Aurora safe from the evil fairy. Maleficent was very powerful, and the good fairies would protect the child. Aurora's parents let the good fairies take the princess to an abandoned woodcutter's cottage in the forest.

For sixteen years, Flora, Fauna, and Merryweather raised the princess as if she were their own daughter. They called her Briar Rose. Since they did not use magic in the house, Briar Rose did not know that her three loving caretakers were really fairies. She also did not know that she was a princess. She lived a humble life and enjoyed growing up among the flowers and animals of the forest. She grew to be a beautiful young woman.

On her sixteenth birthday, the fairies wanted to throw Briar Rose a special party. They planned to make Briar Rose a dress and a special birthday cake, so they sent her into the woods to gather berries.

In addition to being very beautiful, Briar Rose had a lovely singing voice. This was her gift from Fauna. As Briar Rose picked berries, the forest creatures came out to greet her. She sang to them and told them that she had dreamed of meeting a handsome stranger.

As she sang, her voice carried through the forest trees. Prince Phillip, riding through the woods on his horse, Samson, heard the beautiful singing. He was enchanted by Briar Rose's voice.

Samson began galloping through the trees to find the singer. He jumped too high and threw Prince Phillip into a pond. As Prince Phillip took off his cloak and boots to dry, the animals saw him. They guessed that this stranger must be the prince in Briar Rose's dreams. They stole his boots and cloak and led him right to Briar Rose.

When the prince saw Briar Rose, he knew that she was the woman he had to marry. Briar Rose recognized the stranger as the handsome man from her dreams. She promised to meet him that night at the cottage.

When Briar Rose returned to the cottage, Flora, Fauna, and Merryweather surprised her with the cake and new dress. The fairies had decided that it would be all right to use their magic just this once to make the dress and cake as special as possible. Little did they know that Maleficent's evil pet raven was flying above the cottage at that exact moment. The raven knew what was going on immediately. It went back to tell Maleficent that the Princess was still alive.

Briar Rose excitedly told the fairies about the man she met in the woods. The fairies had to explain that she could not marry the stranger because she was really Princess Aurora. She was to marry Prince Phillip. They were to return to the kingdom that day. Aurora was sad.

At the castle, the fairies left the princess alone to rest. Maleficent appeared to Aurora and put her under a spell. Then the evil fairy made a spinning wheel appear. Aurora touched the spindle and, sure enough, she pricked her finger and instantly fell into a deep sleep.

To be sure that Aurora would not be kissed by her true love, Maleficent captured Prince Phillip. She locked him in her dungeon. But Flora, Fauna, and Merryweather managed to rescue Prince Phillip and gave him special weapons to fight the evil of Maleficent. Prince Phillip was challenged by the guards at Maleficent's castle, and then by a thick forest of thorns that Maleficent magically created around Princess Aurora's kingdom. He chopped his way through the thorns. He was almost there when Maleficent appeared and changed into a giant fiery dragon. Phillip used his Sword of Truth to destroy the dragon and get to the Princess.

Princess Aurora was even more beautiful than the first time the Prince met her in the forest. Prince Phillip could not help but bend down and give her a kiss. Aurora awoke from her deep sleep. She could not believe that her true love from the forest was Prince Phillip. They were quickly married and lived a long, happy life together.

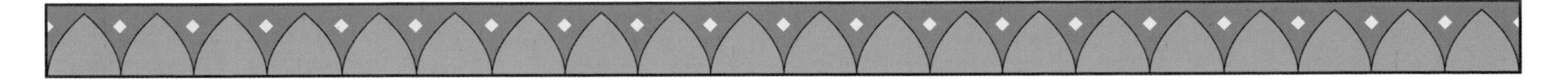

Aladdin

Story adapted by Lisa Harkrader

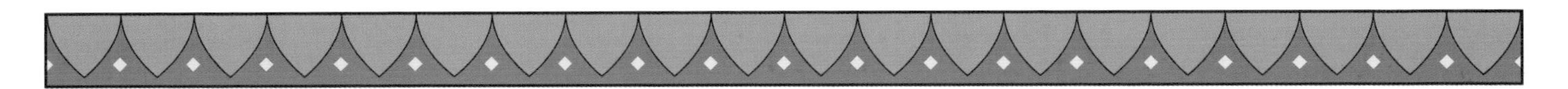

Jafar was the Sultan's most trusted advisor. However, the Sultan did not realize that Jafar had evil plans.

Jafar wanted a magic lamp that was hidden deep in the Cave of Wonders. With the power of the lamp, he could become Sultan.

The cave would only allow one person to enter. This mysterious person was called a "diamond in the rough." If anyone else stepped foot inside, the Cave of Wonders would collapse into the desert sands.

"I must find this diamond in the rough," Jafar told Iago, his parrot. "And I know how."

Jafar found the Sultan in the garden with the princess. Another prince had just left the palace in a huff.

"Jasmine," said the Sultan, "you must stop rejecting every suitor who comes to call. The law says you must be married to a prince."

"But, Father, I don't like these princes," said Jasmine. "If I marry, I'll marry for love."

Jafar offered to help the Sultan. "I'll need your Mystique Blue Diamond to do so, though," he lied.

The Sultan fell for the trick and gave Jafar his blue diamond ring. With the ring, Jafar could see an image of the diamond in the rough. He was a street urchin named Aladdin.

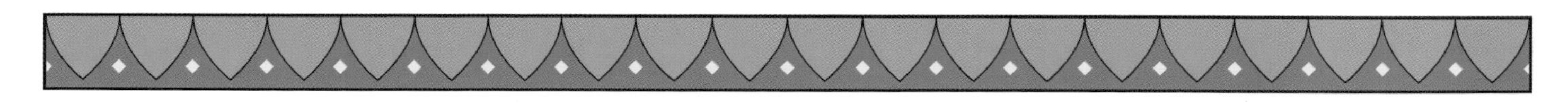

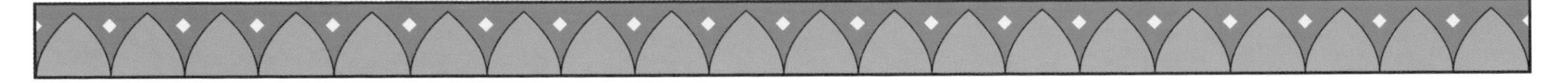

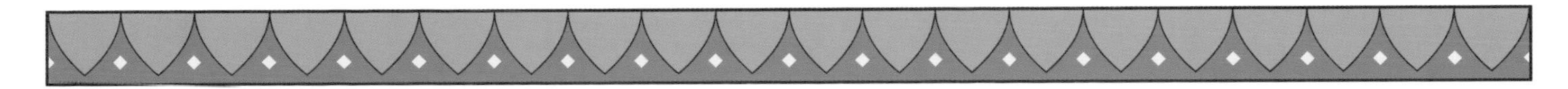

Meanwhile, Princess Jasmine thought to herself, "I've never done anything on my own. I've never even been outside the palace walls."

So Jasmine disguised herself as a peasant. She snuck out of the palace and into the city. In the marketplace, she met Aladdin and his pet monkey, Abu. Aladdin liked Jasmine immediately and showed her around the city. Jasmine loved the view from the rooftops.

Jafar had sent soldiers to arrest Aladdin. Jasmine couldn't stop them. The soldiers took Aladdin to the palace and threw him in the dungeon.

Another prisoner in the dungeon told Aladdin about the Cave of Wonders. "It's filled with enough treasure to impress a princess," he said. "I need someone young like you to help me get it."

The prisoner showed Aladdin a secret escape route from the dungeon. Aladdin didn't know that the prisoner was Jafar in disguise.

When Aladdin and Jafar reached the Cave of Wonders, the cave spoke to Aladdin. "You're the diamond in the rough. You may enter. But take nothing but the lamp."

Inside the cave, Aladdin and Abu found mountains of gold and jewels. They also found a magic flying carpet. The carpet was like a real person. It was very friendly and led them to the lamp, perched high on a mound of stones. Aladdin climbed the stones to the lamp.

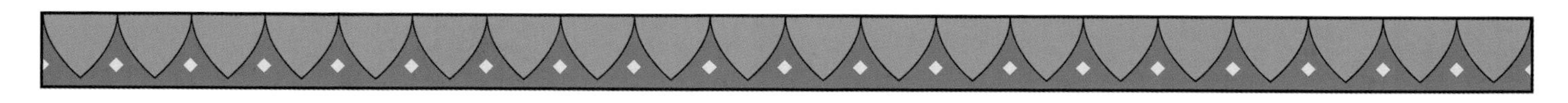

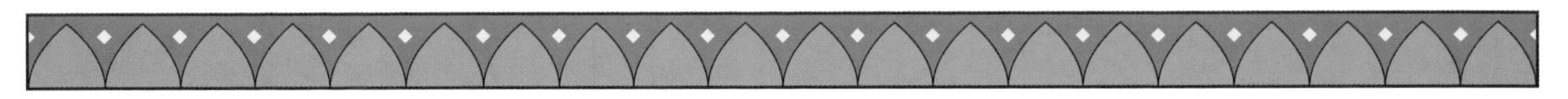

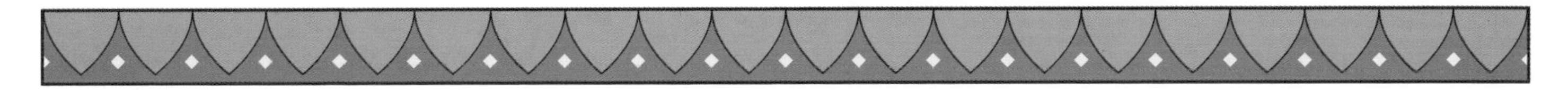

As Aladdin grabbed the lamp, Abu grabbed a jewel.

The ground trembled. "You have touched forbidden treasure," roared the voice of the cave. "You'll never again see the light of day."

The cave shook. As rocks fell from the ceiling, the treasure melted into a flaming pool of gold. Aladdin and Abu swooped forward through the cave on the Magic Carpet. Before they could fly out, a rock fell onto the carpet and sent Aladdin hurtling off. He clung to the side of the cave, just inches from where they came in. Jafar was waiting and seized the lamp. Aladdin fell back into the cave. Before the cave collapsed beneath the desert, Abu snatched the lamp from Jafar and scampered back to Aladdin.

Aladdin, Abu, and the Magic Carpet found themselves trapped inside the cave. "All for this stupid lamp," said Aladdin. He rubbed the lamp, and a blue genie spewed from its spout.

"I've been in that lamp ten thousand years," said the genie. "Since you released me from the lamp, you're now my master. I'll grant you three wishes."

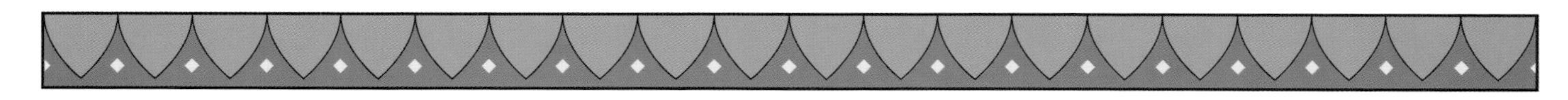

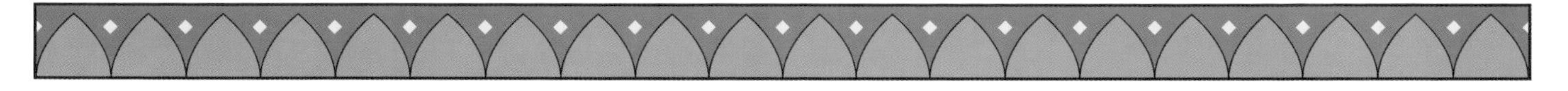

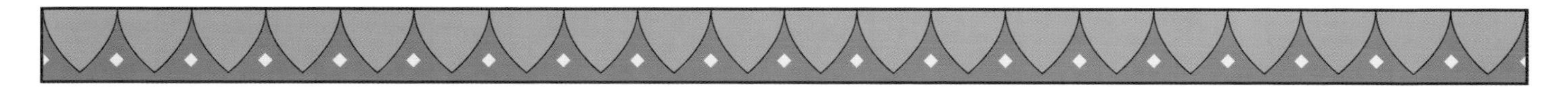

Before Aladdin could make a wish, the Genie burst through the roof of the cave. He, Aladdin, and Abu flew over the desert on the Magic Carpet.

It was time for Aladdin to make his first wish. "What would you wish for?" he asked the Genie.

"That's easy," said Genie. "I'd wish to be free, to be my own master. But that can't happen unless one of my masters uses a wish to wish me free. And nobody wants to waste a wish on that."

"I will," said Aladdin. "After I make my first two wishes, I'll use my third to set you free. And I know what my first wish will be. Genie, I wish to be a prince."

So the Genie turned Aladdin into a prince. He dressed Aladdin in princely clothes. He gave Aladdin princely riches and turned Abu into a royal elephant. Aladdin rode Abu to the palace, surrounded by soldiers, camels, peacocks, and lions.

Aladdin called himself Prince Ali. He tried to impress Jasmine with his wealth. But Jasmine didn't think Prince Ali was any different from all the other dull and arrogant princes who had come to call. She didn't know that he was the boy she had met in the market.

So Aladdin took Jasmine for a ride on the Magic Carpet. He showed Jasmine the city at night. He acted like himself, rather than like a stuffy prince, and Jasmine kissed him.

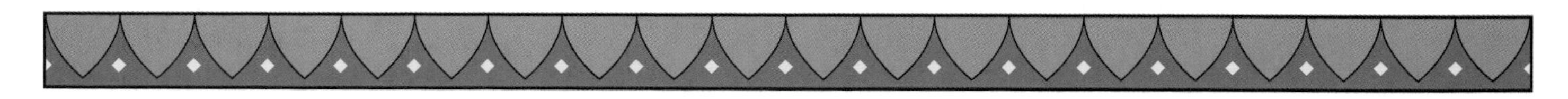

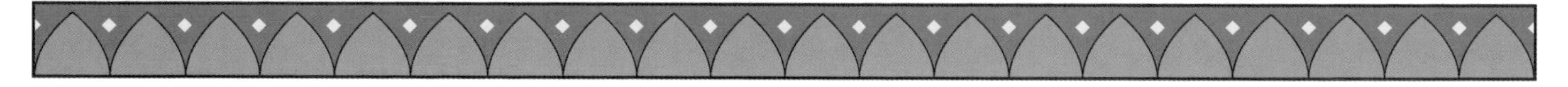

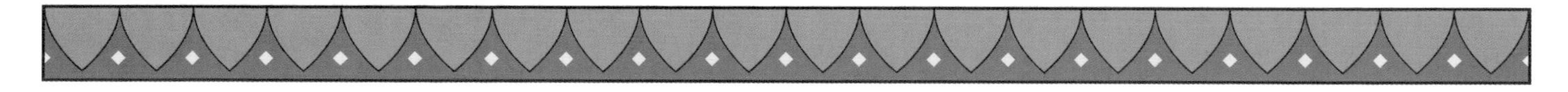

Jafar saw that Jasmine was falling in love with Prince Ali. Not knowing that they were the same person, Jafar ordered the palace guards to capture Aladdin. The guards tied Aladdin up and threw him into the ocean.

Aladdin used his second wish to ask Genie to save his life, and Genie did. Shortly after, Jasmine told her father she wanted to marry Prince Ali.

But Jafar realized that Prince Ali was really Aladdin. He also knew that Aladdin had the magic lamp. He sent Iago to Aladdin's room to steal the lamp. Jafar rubbed the lamp. The Genie puffed out of the spout.

"Hey, you're not Aladdin," said the Genie.

"No," said Jafar. "But I'm your master now, and you will grant me three wishes. For my first wish, I wish for you to make me the Sultan who rules from the sky."

The Genie had no choice. He turned Jafar into the Sultan. He ripped the palace from the desert sand and placed it on a mountaintop so that Jafar could rule from the sky. Jafar then turned Jasmine and her father into helpless slaves.

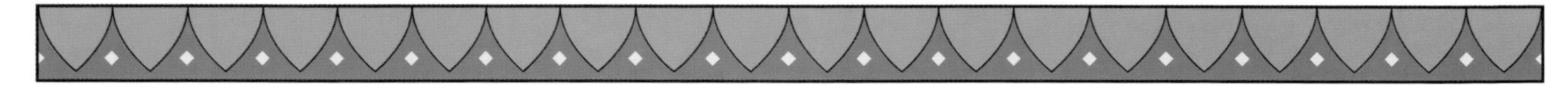

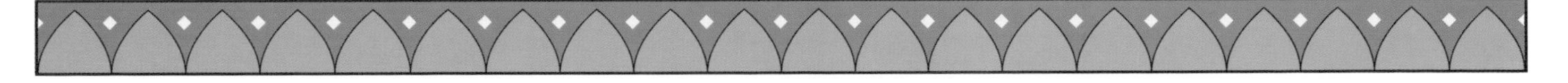

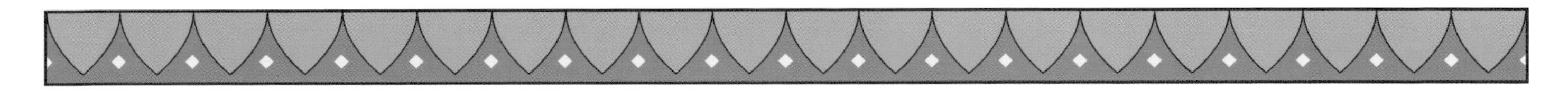

Now that Jafar was the Genie's master, Aladdin couldn't ask for his last wish. Aladdin lost his princely riches, and Abu turned back into a monkey. Jafar banished them, along with the Magic Carpet, to the ends of the earth.

But Aladdin would not give up. "I'll find a way to stop Jafar," he said.

Aladdin and Abu rode the Magic Carpet back to the palace. Aladdin attacked Jafar with a sword, but Jafar easily fought him off. Jafar realized he could have even more power.

"Why should I stop at being Sultan?" he said. "Genie, for my second wish, make me the world's most powerful sorcerer."

The Genie had no choice. He turned Jafar into the world's most powerful sorcerer. Aladdin knew he couldn't fight a sorcerer with a sword. He had to trick him.

"You may be the most powerful sorcerer in the world," Aladdin told Jafar, "but you're not the most powerful being. Genie is a hundred times more powerful than you."

"You're right." Jafar smiled. "And I have one wish left. Genie, make me a genie as powerful as you."

"He's your master, Genie," said Aladdin. "You must grant his wish."

So the Genie turned Jafar into a huge, powerful genie.

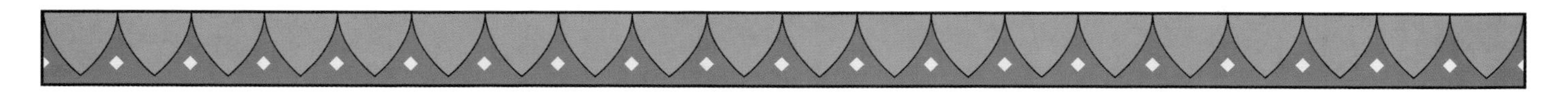

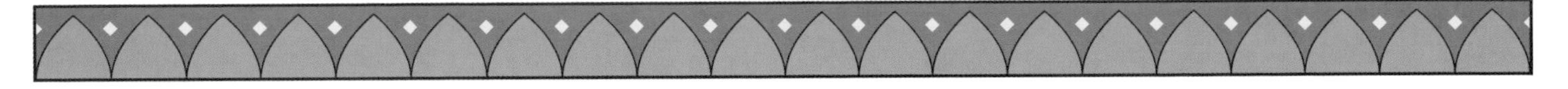

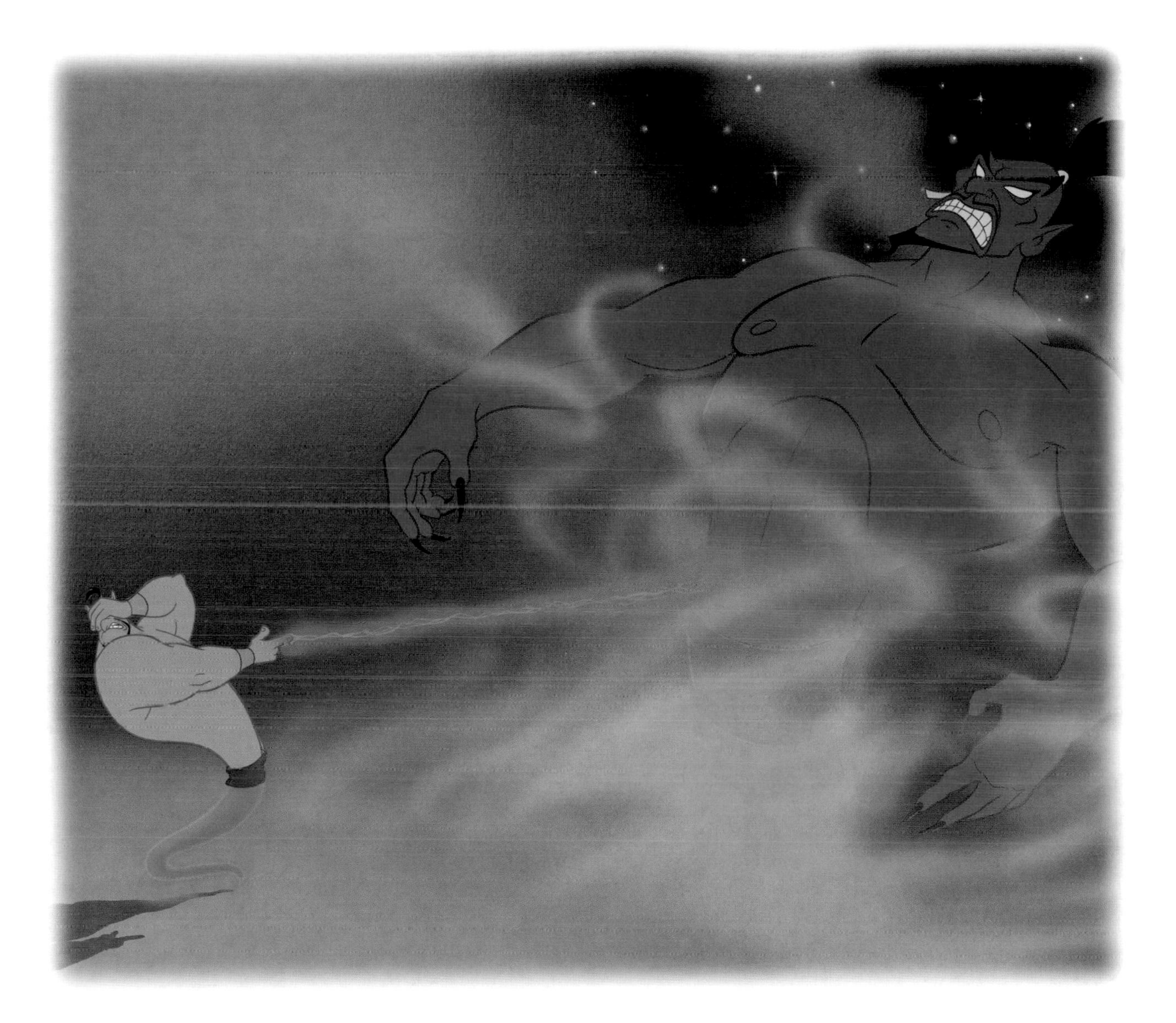

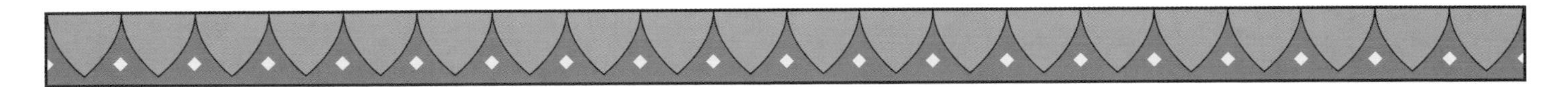

"I'm the most powerful being in the world!" cried Jafar.

But genies live inside lamps, and Jafar's lamp was small and black. It sucked Jafar into its spout.

Aladdin looked at Genie. "He's stuck unless somebody rubs his lamp."

"And I'm not going to let that happen," said Genie. He hurled Jafar's lamp over the balcony into the desert and toward the Cave of Wonders.

"You have one wish," said Genie. "Shall I make you a prince again?"

Aladdin shook his head. "I promised I'd use my last wish to set you free. I'm sorry, Jasmine. I love you, but I can't pretend to be a prince. I can't pretend to be something I'm not. Genie, I wish you to be free."

In a puff, Genie became free.

"Now we can never be married," said Jasmine.

"Nonsense," said Jasmine's father. "I'm the Sultan! I can change the law. From now on, the princess shall marry whomever she chooses."

"And I choose Aladdin," said Jasmine. "I choose Aladdin!"

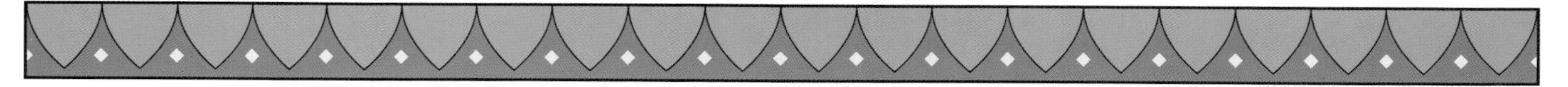

ROBIN HOOD

Story adapted by Lora Kalkman

Robin Hood and Little John lived in Sherwood Forest, near the town of Nottingham. The two friends were considered heroes by most people. They robbed from the rich to give to the poor. Evil Prince John made poor people pay enormously unfair taxes. Robin Hood and Little John just took the money back and gave it to its rightful owners.

The taxes were collected by the Sheriff of Nottingham, who was especially rotten. He took children's birthday money to give to Prince John!

It hadn't always been that way. Prince John's brother, King Richard, had been a kind and noble king. Unfortunately, King Richard was away from the kingdom. He was off fighting on a crusade.

One day, Robin Hood and Little John heard a trumpet sound.

Peering through the trees, they noticed Prince John's royal carriage approaching.

Robin Hood grinned and rubbed his hands together. "That sounds like another collection day for the poor," he said gleefully.

Robin Hood and Little John devised a plan. Quickly, they dressed up as fortune-tellers and hid along the path.

"Ooo-da-lolly, ooo-da-lolly," called Robin Hood in a disguised voice. "Fortunes forecast!" announced Little John.

Prince John was amused. He wanted to have his fortune told and ordered the carriage to stop. Prince John's servant, Sir Hiss, warned the Prince that the fortune-tellers might be bandits.

"Rubbish," said the Prince, and he motioned the fortune-tellers toward his carriage.

Robin Hood and Little John seized the opportunity. First, when Prince John encouraged them to kiss his royal hand, they stole the gems from his rings! When Sir Hiss tried to tell the prince what had happened, he was stuffed into a basket.

Later, Little John filled a globe with fireflies. Robin Hood treated the globe like a crystal ball and pretended to reveal the future. Then he swiped Prince John's gold and his royal cloak. Outside, Little John stole even more, including the golden hubcaps from the royal coach.

When Prince John realized what had happened, he was shocked. "Mommy," he whimpered. Then he sucked his thumb. He knew he'd been hoodwinked by Robin Hood.

Prince John was outraged at Robin Hood. He summoned the evil Sheriff of Nottingham for help.

The villains knew Robin Hood was an excellent archer, so they decided to hold an archery contest. They planned to capture Robin Hood at the event. To ensure Robin Hood would attend, the Prince promised the winner a kiss from Maid Marian. He knew Robin Hood liked her, for they once were sweethearts.

Sure enough, Robin Hood attended the contest. He came disguised as a stork with long, spindly legs and a huge beak. At first, no one but Maid Marian recognized the dashing rogue. Everyone cheered for the stranger, who proved to be an excellent archer.

In the final round of competition, the Sheriff resorted to cheating. Just as the stork made his final shot, the Sheriff bumped him, and the arrow went astray. Robin Hood was not deterred. He quickly fired another arrow and heroically won the competition.

Prince John realized only Robin Hood could have made such an incredible shot. When the stork went to collect his prize kiss, Prince John revealed his disguise. “Seize him!” Prince John ordered, and Robin Hood was captured.

Fortunately, Little John came to the rescue, and Robin Hood was freed. A crazy battle ensued. The townspeople helped Robin Hood, Little John, and Maid Marian escape into the woods.

Prince John was furious. The townspeople cheered for their hero. That made the Prince angrier still. He raised taxes even more.

When people could not pay their taxes, they were put in jail. Nasty Prince John even put children in jail!

Friar Tuck was a kindly fellow. But when the Sheriff took his last coin, Friar Tuck was outraged. “Get out of my church!” he shouted. But the Sheriff arrested Friar Tuck and put him in jail, too.

That gave Prince John an idea. He announced that he would punish Friar Tuck in the morning, knowing Robin Hood would come to the rescue. He ordered his guards to seize Robin Hood then!

When Robin Hood learned of the planned punishment, he had to act quickly.

That night, Robin Hood and Little John snuck into the castle. The Sheriff of Nottingham was keeping guard. Robin Hood disguised himself as one of Prince John's helpers and tricked the Sheriff. Before long, he coaxed the Sheriff to sleep. Then Robin Hood took the jail key and gave it to Little John. Little John rescued Friar Tuck and all the others.

Meanwhile, Robin Hood snuck into Prince John's room. He planned to take all of Prince John's gold.

When Prince John awoke, he realized what was happening. The guards chased Robin Hood and trapped him inside the castle. Robin Hood climbed tall gates and scaled high walls. He swung from ropes and dodged dozens of arrows to get away. When the Sheriff accidentally set the castle on fire, Robin Hood jumped into the moat. His friends watched breathlessly from the woods to see whether their hero would escape.

When Robin Hood's cap floated to the top of the moat, his friends feared the worst. Then they spotted a reed gliding toward shore. Before long, Robin Hood emerged from the moat. The hero had gotten away! "Ooo-da-lolly!" he shouted, and his friends rejoiced.

Prince John could hardly believe his eyes. He was quite upset, to be sure. When Hiss pointed out that the castle was in flames, Prince John was even more upset. "Mommy," he whimpered. Then he sucked his thumb.

Back in Nottingham, the townspeople were happy to have their money back. They were even happier to learn that King Richard had returned. When the good king came back, he locked up the Sheriff, Prince John, Sir Hiss, and all of the prince's evil helpers.

Meanwhile, Robin Hood and Maid Marian had a joyous wedding. All of the townspeople were invited to the celebration. Friar Tuck and King Richard were there as well. "Long live Robin Hood!" everyone shouted as the wedding bells rang.

After the ceremony, Little John ushered Robin Hood and his bride into their carriage. The townspeople wished the happy couple well as they rode away. Nottingham was a happy place once again.

Bambi
Story adapted by Gayla Amaral

Yawn! It was time for Friend Owl to sleep. The sun was coming up, and the forest creatures were waking up. Just as he nodded off, a bluebird began to chirp the wonderful news—a prince had come into the world!

"It isn't every day a new prince is born," said Friend Owl, following the other animals through the woods.

There in the thicket he lay—a newly born fawn nestled next to his mother. The crowd of forest creatures gathered around, making a fuss over him as he wobbled to his feet.

"Whatcha gonna call him?" asked Thumper, a friendly little bunny.

"I think I'll call him Bambi," the mother replied, nuzzling her baby.

Soon Bambi was ready to explore the forest. With help from Thumper, Bambi learned to hop, skip, jump, and even talk!

"Bird!" Bambi said. He proudly used his first new word to describe everything in sight.

"That's not a bird," said Thumper giggling. "That's a butterfly."

"Flower!" exclaimed Bambi upon discovering a little skunk hiding in a flower bed.

Thumper laughed. It seemed funny to call a skunk "Flower."

"He can call me 'Flower' if he wants to," said the baby skunk, liking his new name.

One morning, Bambi's mother led him to the meadow. Thumper had told him that they weren't the only deer in the forest, so Bambi was eager to rush into the meadow and meet the others. But his mother stopped him with a warning: "Never rush out into the meadow. There might be danger."

When his mother announced that they were safe, Bambi ran all over the meadow. He was fascinated with his reflection in the brook and became startled when he saw a second fawn gazing into it as well. The bashful Bambi fell all over himself to get away. His playful new friend, Faline, thought his shyness was cute and chased after him.

All around him deer were running and leaping. Bambi noticed one buck in particular. As the majestic deer walked by, he stopped to take a long look at Bambi.

"Who is that?" Bambi asked his mother.

"He's the Great Prince of the Forest," she replied. "He's very brave and wise and has lived a long time." Bambi was in awe of the Great Prince. He hoped to grow up to be a great prince, too.

Suddenly, the Great Prince heard something. Warning the other deer of approaching danger, he ran with them from the meadow.

After reaching safety, Bambi asked, "Why were we running?"

"Man was in the forest," his mother answered solemnly.

As autumn leaves turned to snow and ice, Bambi enjoyed his first winter. Making tracks in the snow was fun, until he sank into a snowdrift. Suddenly, Thumper came hopping by.

"The water is frozen!" said Thumper, skating smoothly across the ice.

"Yippee!" shouted Bambi, attempting to follow Thumper. He wasn't as graceful as Thumper and slid across the ice. Thumper did his best to push and pull Bambi to his feet, but couldn't stop them both from sliding into a tree trunk where a sleeping Flower lay hibernating for the winter.

In spite of the fun, winter seemed to last forever. One day, Bambi's mother found a patch of grass, the first sign of the coming spring.

Bambi was just beginning to enjoy the delicious grass when he heard his mother cry, "Quick, Bambi, hunters! Run! Run and don't look back!"

They ran from the hunters as fast as they could. Reaching safety, Bambi sighed, "We made it, Mother!" But she was nowhere to be found. It was time for Bambi to be on his own.

Tweet! Tweet! The birds of the forest announced the arrival of spring.

"Hello, Friend Owl!" said Bambi to his old friend. "It's been a while. Don't you remember me?"

"Oh, my! How you've changed!" exclaimed the owl. "I see you've traded in your spots for a pair of antlers."

Thump! Thump! It was Thumper, and close behind him was Flower! The three friends had grown into handsome young creatures and were excited to see each other again.

Spring was glorious, but Friend Owl warned them, "You never know when you'll run smack into a pretty face—and then you'll be twitterpated!"

"Twitterpated?" questioned the three friends. "What's twitterpated?"

"You feel weak in the knees," answered the owl, "and your head's in a whirl. You feel like you're walking on air!" None of the three believed that they would be twitterpated, but no sooner had Friend Owl spoken than Flower and Thumper were both smitten by love. Then Bambi heard a voice.

"Hello! Don't you remember me?" said Faline. She was absolutely beautiful, and Bambi fell head over heels in love!

Bambi and Faline spent the beginning of the spring frolicking through the forest. They would run among the trees, and smell the flowers. When they stopped for a drink at the creek, Faline gave Bambi a kiss on the cheek.

Bambi and Faline had a wonderful time. Everything seemed perfect. One day, however, the Great Prince and Bambi stood high on a cliff watching smoke rise from a hunter's campfire.

"It is Man," the Great Prince said to Bambi. "We all must go deeper into the forest." Bambi heard the hunters and their dogs getting closer and closer. Thanks to Bambi, Faline escaped. But Bambi was injured as he ran from the hunters.

Meanwhile, the hunters' campfire began to burn out of control. Soon the flames spread toward the part of the forest where Bambi lay injured.

"Get up! Get up!" the Great Prince urged Bambi. "Come with me," he ordered as he led Bambi away from the fire. The flames were everywhere and followed closely behind them. The other animals were on the run as well, including Faline, Thumper, and Flower. Bambi and the Great Prince ran through the brook and found themselves with no choice but to jump over a waterfall to escape the burning fire.

As the Great Prince and Bambi swam ashore, Bambi was thrilled and relieved to find that Faline was safe as well. They looked sadly around them. Everything was burned and scorched.

It was a sad day for the animals. The forest was a burnt shadow of what it had been just yesterday. Thankfully, no one was badly hurt.

The seasons passed, and the scorched forest came to life once more.

Thump! Thump! Thump! "Wake up! Wake up!" exclaimed Thumper. He and his four little bunnies woke Friend Owl with their excited thumping.

"It's happened in the thicket," added Flower excitedly. A prince had been born! The forest animals couldn't wait to see the new arrival. They remembered when the last prince, their friend Bambi, had been born.

"Oh, my! Oh, my!" they exclaimed in unison. They could hardly believe their eyes. Two adorable fawns stood wobbling together at the feet of their mother and father, who were none other than Bambi and Faline.

"I don't believe I've ever seen a more likely-looking pair," said the raccoon. Everyone agreed, of course, especially Thumper and Flower.

Friend Owl agreed, "Prince Bambi must be very proud!" he exclaimed.

Friend Owl was right. Bambi was very proud indeed.

Hercules

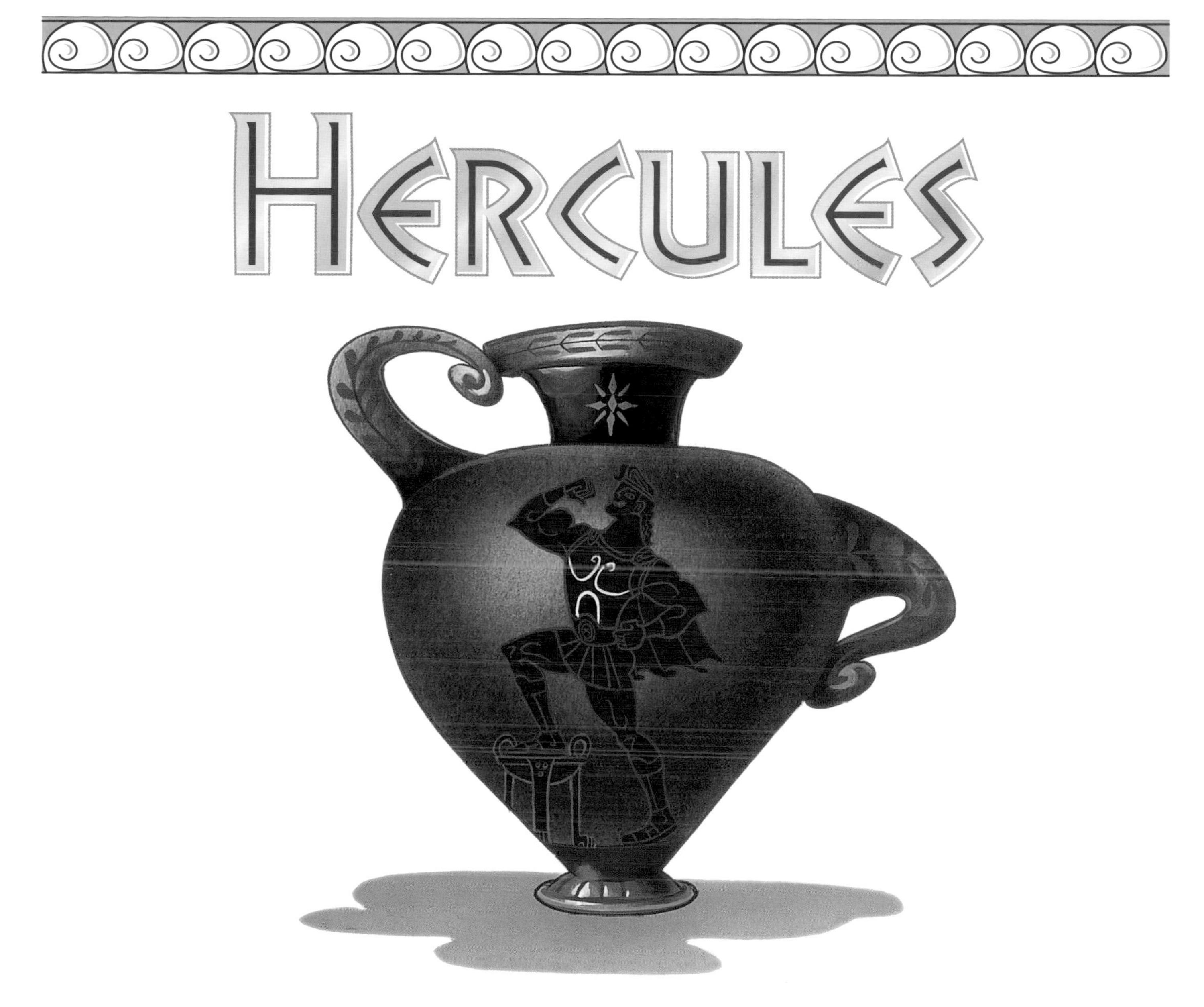

Story adapted by Lora Kalkman

High atop the tremendous Mt. Olympus lived all the great Gods of Greece. Their mighty leader, Zeus, was married to the lovely Hera. Gods who lived on Mt. Olympus were immortal, meaning they could live forever. The Gods were all heroes to the people of Greece.

Hera and Zeus welcomed a baby boy into the world. It was a joyous day for all the residents of Mt. Olympus. The couple named their baby Hercules. As the son of mighty Zeus, Hercules inherited his father's strength. Zeus extended his finger to tickle his son's cheek, only to have the tiny Hercules grab his finger and pick Zeus up off the ground. Zeus was very proud of his little boy's strength.

At a grand celebration held to honor the arrival of Hercules, all the immortals who lived on Mt. Olympus came with gifts for the child. Zeus had a very special gift for his boy. He gave Hercules a flying baby horse named Pegasus. Hercules and Pegasus adored each other instantly.

But suddenly, a dark shadowy figure appeared at the party. His name was Hades, and he was the evil ruler of the Underworld. Hades tried to give Hercules a rattle with dangerous spikes. Wise little Hercules could tell right away that Hades was a rotten villain, so he bit Hades on the finger.

Unbeknownst to the others, Hades had an evil plan. He was preparing to overthrow Zeus and take over the world. Hades would soon learn, however, that little Hercules was to be his biggest nemesis.

Back in the Underworld, Hades called upon the Fates. The Fates were very wise and could see into the future. Hades asked for their help, using flattering compliments to win them over. The Fates, having fallen for Hades's evil charm, warned him that Hercules would be the one who could stop Hades from ruling the world.

"A word of caution to this tale," they said all together. "Should Hercules fight, you will fail."

Hades knew that Hercules would remain very strong and powerful as long as he was immortal. Hades prepared a potion that would change Hercules from immortal to mortal. Then he sent his flying henchmen, Pain and Panic, to take the baby and feed him the potion.

When Zeus discovered his son was missing, he created a huge, angry thunderstorm. Pain and Panic, who had been soaring through the sky with the baby Hercules, plummeted back to earth. Hercules was unharmed, but the henchmen quickly fed him the bottle of potion. They knew he had to drink every last drop for the potion to work completely.

Just as Hercules was about to finish the bottle, a kind man and woman happened by. Pain and Panic were startled by the couple and quickly scurried away. The bottle fell and broke before little Hercules had finished the last drop.

The kind couple scooped up the tiny baby and took him home.

The little infant wore a gold medallion around his neck that said "Hercules" above the image of a lightning bolt. The couple felt that this baby needed a family, so they raised Hercules as if he were their own son.

Hercules grew up to be very strong. In fact, Hercules once pulled his father's haycart into the village after their donkey hurt its leg. Aside from that, he actually pulled the wagon faster than any donkey ever could.

Hercules' strength often got him into trouble. Once, while playing catch with friends, he leaped to make a fantastic grab. Hercules lost his balance and bumped into a stone column. The entire building crumbled to the ground because of Hercules's clumsiness.

As time passed, the other kids did not want to play with him. They were afraid of his strength.

Hercules began to feel like an outcast. He tried so hard to fit in, but he just couldn't.

"Sometimes I feel like I really don't belong here, like I'm supposed to be someplace else," he told his father.

Hercules's parents showed him the medallion he had worn as a baby. He recognized the bolt of lightning as the symbol of Zeus and felt compelled to learn more about the medallion. He made a trip to the temple of Zeus.

The temple was magnificent. Hercules looked around in awe. In the center of the temple was a giant statue of Zeus. Without warning, the statue came to life. Hercules started to run, but Zeus picked him right up.

"After all these years," bellowed Zeus, "is this the kind of hello you give your father?"

Zeus went on to explain all that had happened to Hercules. He also explained to Hercules that he could return to Mt. Olympus only if he proved himself a true hero on Earth.

Zeus told the boy to seek out Philoctetes, the Trainer of Heroes. He would help Hercules become a true hero. Finally, before he left the temple, Zeus reunited Hercules with his flying horse, Pegasus.

Hercules found Philoctetes. "Call me Phil," said the Trainer. Hercules persuaded Phil to become his trainer. They worked on many, many skills until finally, Hercules was ready to test his strength. He was going to the city of Thebes to be a hero.

Hercules heard the cries of a woman in distress. He rushed to her aid and defeated her captor. Hercules learned that the woman's name was Megara, or Meg for short, and he fell in love with her immediately.

What Hercules didn't realize was that Meg worked for Hades.

When Meg reported back, Hades became furious that Hercules was still alive and very powerful. He needed a plan to get rid of Hercules. He sent Meg to lure him into a trap. Meg had fallen for Hercules, too, but was indebted to Hades and had to follow his orders.

Meanwhile, the townspeople gathered around as Hercules was about to help two little boys who were trapped in a cave. The townspeople cheered when Hercules freed them. Nobody was aware that the boys were really Pain and Panic in disguise. Suddenly, a mean, giant, purple monster emerged from the cave. When Hercules valiantly fought it off, the townspeople cheered again. But the battle was not over.

Every time Hercules thought he had defeated the purple monster, a new head would grow from its body. Soon Hercules was surrounded by dozens of evil purple heads. Hercules jumped aboard Pegasus and drew his sword, but the monsters soon cornered him. Hercules thought quickly. Noticing the giant stone mountain nearby, he smashed his fist into it. Hercules's strength sent an avalanche tumbling down onto the monster and all its heads.

The townspeople celebrated. Hercules was their hero. Meg was very impressed. As the months passed, Hercules became known throughout the land as the greatest hero of all time. For the first time ever, Hercules was treated like a king.

Hercules had foiled Hades's attempt to destroy him. But Hades realized that Hercules's weakness was Meg. Hercules would do anything for her. Hades made a deal with Meg. He would free her if she would help him.

Meanwhile, Hercules went to see Zeus. Zeus said that although he was famous, Hercules had not yet proven himself a true hero. "What more can I do?" asked Hercules. Zeus replied, "It's something you must discover for yourself. Look inside your heart to discover what you must do."

When Hades came to remind Meg of her mission, Phil overheard. Phil told Hercules that Meg was a fraud, but Hercules refused to believe him. Before Phil could convince him, Hades appeared. He had a deal to make.

In exchange for Meg's safety, Hercules would have to give up his powers for twenty-four hours. That would give Hades time to take over the world.

Hercules agreed. Hades was thrilled and unleashed the Titans from their underground prison. The battle with Zeus began. A giant one-eyed monster was sent to get Hercules.

In all the commotion, a stone column began to fall. Meg pushed Hercules out of the way, but the column landed on her. The deal Hercules made with Hades was supposed to keep Meg safe. Since she was hurt, the deal was broken. All of Hercules' strength was returned to him.

Hercules was able to rescue Zeus, who had been captured, and together they succeeded in conquering all of the evil Titans.

Having escaped, Hades grabbed Meg and took her back to the Underworld. Hercules followed them. He announced that he was willing to sacrifice his life to save Meg. This selfless act of love proved he was a true hero. Hades was defeated and Hercules' immortality was restored.

Hercules was able to return home to Mt. Olympus. He soon realized, however, that his place was with Meg, whom he loved. Happily, he returned to Earth. Hercules and Meg lived their lives happily ever after.

Story adapted by Amy Adair

Ariel, the daughter of the mighty King Triton, was swimming through an old shipwreck with her friend, Flounder. Ariel liked to collect things that belonged to humans.

"What do you think this is?" Ariel asked, holding up a fork. Flounder shook his head. He had never seen anything like it.

Ariel was sure her friend Scuttle the seagull would know what this strange and wonderful thing was. He lived on land and knew all about the human world. Ariel and Flounder swam to the surface.

Scuttle carefully examined the fork. "It's a dinglehopper," he said. "Humans use it to straighten their hair."

Ursula, the evil sea witch, had been gazing into her magic ball. Ursula watched Ariel as she explored the ocean. Long ago, King Triton had banished Ursula from his kingdom and she wanted revenge. She knew King Triton would do anything for his precious daughter.

"Ariel just might be the key to King Triton's undoing," Ursula laughed.

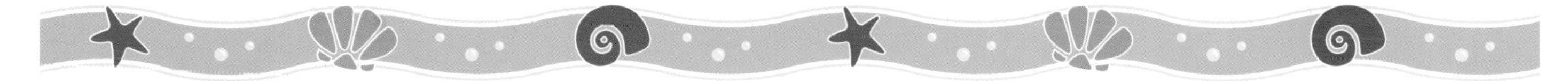

Ariel returned home to find her father waiting for her. King Triton was angry. He found out that Ariel had gone up to the surface. He didn't trust humans and going to the surface was too risky for any mermaid or merman. He told Ariel never to go above the sea again. Ariel was very upset. She cried and swam away. More than anything, Ariel wanted to be part of the human world.

As she swam away, King Triton ordered his loyal friend Sebastian, a crab, to follow Ariel. He wanted to make sure that she stayed out of trouble.

Before Sebastian could catch up to her, Ariel saw the bottom of a ship. She raced to the surface. She watched as the men celebrated Prince Eric's birthday. Scuttle flew over the sea and spotted Ariel.

"Look at Prince Eric," Ariel whispered to Scuttle. "Isn't he handsome?"

Suddenly, the winds changed. "A hurricane is coming!" a sailor yelled.

All the sailors jumped safely into a lifeboat. But Prince Eric's dog, Max, was stranded on the ship. Eric climbed back onto the sinking ship. He put Max safely in a lifeboat, but Eric sank with the ship to the bottom of the sea. Ariel dove down after him and pulled him to the shore.

"I'd give anything to stay here beside him," Ariel told Scuttle.

Ariel sang to Eric until he started to wake up. Then she dove back into the sea, but not before Prince Eric caught a glimpse of her face. He had fallen in love with the stranger with the beautiful voice.

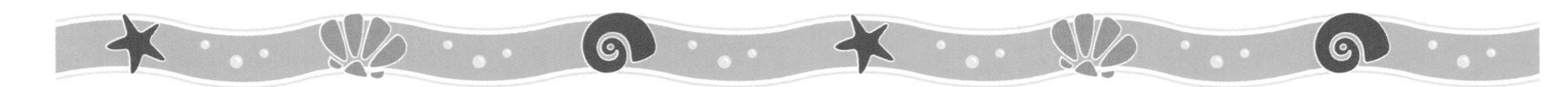

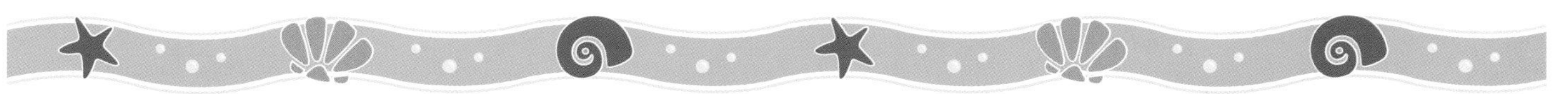

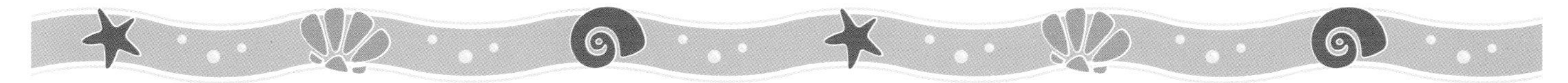

One day, Ursula's eels, Flotsam and Jetsam, visited Ariel.

"Ursula can make all your dreams come true," Flotsam hissed.

"Just imagine you and the prince together forever," Jetsam said.

Ariel was scared. But she followed the eels back to Ursula's cave.

"Come here, my child," Ursula said. "You must become human to make the prince fall in love with you. I can turn you into a human for three days. But the prince must kiss you before the sun sets on the third day. If he does, you'll remain human forever. If not, you'll turn back into a mermaid and belong to me. Your beautiful voice will be my payment."

Ariel gulped and then agreed. As she sang, Ursula captured Ariel's voice in a magic seashell.

Then Ariel's tail disappeared. Sebastian and Flounder grabbed her and raced up to the surface.

Ariel examined her legs and wiggled her toes.

Scuttle flew overhead. "You look different," he said. "Have you been using the dinglehopper?" Ariel laughed silently, then stood up for the first time.

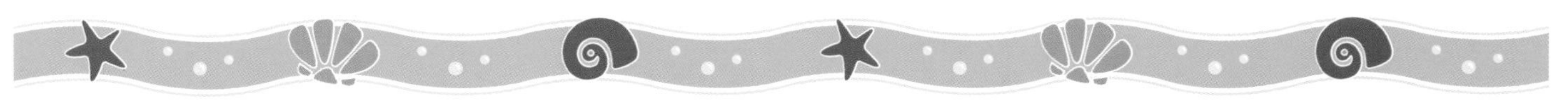

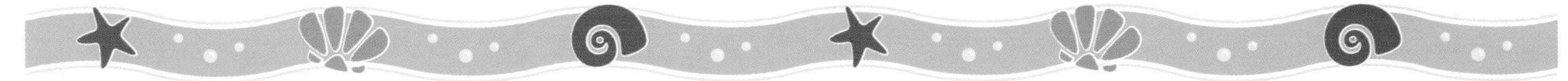

It wasn't long before Prince Eric and Max found Ariel. Prince Eric was sure she was the mysterious stranger with the beautiful voice he had been searching for. "Are you okay?" Eric asked.

Ariel nodded her head.

"You can't speak," Prince Eric said disappointed. "Then you can't be who I thought you were."

Prince Eric took Ariel back to his palace. After a day of exploring the kingdom, Prince Eric and Ariel went for a romantic boat ride on a beautiful lagoon. Sebastian started getting nervous since Prince Eric hadn't kissed Ariel yet. So he set the mood with a romantic tune. Sebastian sang in Eric's ear as the birds, frogs and other creatures sang along.

Eric was falling in love with Ariel. He stared into her eyes.

Ursula watched the couple in her magic ball. She could see that Prince Eric was falling in love with Ariel. Things were not going as she had planned. As Prince Eric leaned in to kiss Ariel, Ursula's eels tipped the boat.

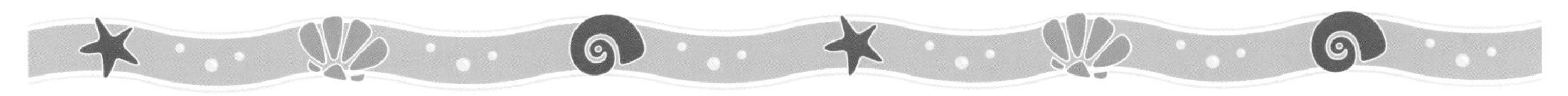

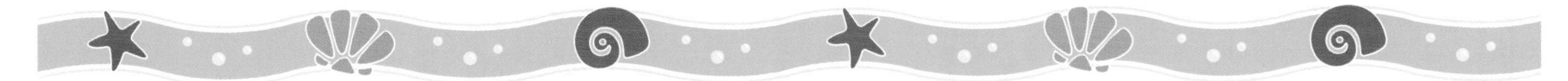

Scuttle woke Ariel the next morning. "You did it!" he said. "The whole town is talking about the prince's wedding!"

Ariel raced to Eric, but he was standing next to another girl whose name was Vanessa. Ariel overheard him say that he wanted to marry Vanessa on a ship at sunset.

Ariel watched sadly as Eric sailed away with Vanessa. She was sure she had lost her prince forever.

Scuttle still thought Ariel was Eric's bride. He flew to the wedding ship to wish her luck. But when he peeked in the window he didn't see Ariel. Instead, he saw Ursula admiring herself in the mirror. The sea witch had tricked the prince. She had disguised herself as Vanessa and had used Ariel's voice.

Scuttle flew back to Ariel and told her what he had seen. Flounder helped Ariel swim to the boat. Meanwhile, Scuttle called all of his friends.

They got there just as Vanessa and Eric were marching down the aisle. Scuttle's friends poured water on Vanessa and pulled her hair. The seashell that Ursula had around her neck fell and broke. It had Ariel's voice trapped inside. When Ariel got her voice back, she began to sing.

Eric turned to Ariel. "You're the one!" he cried. He leaned in to kiss her just as the sun set.

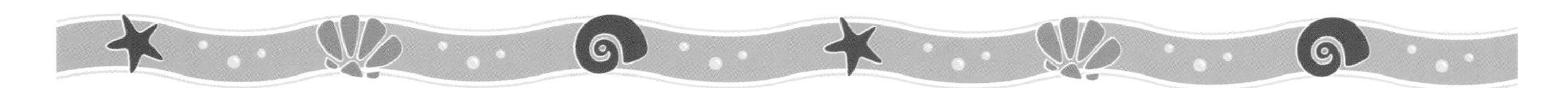

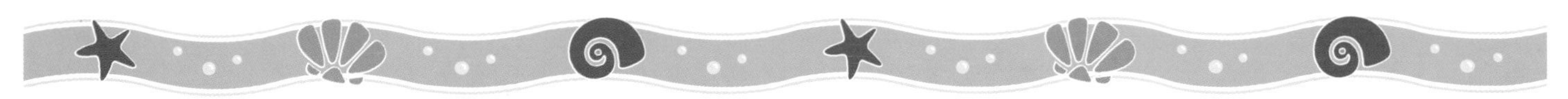

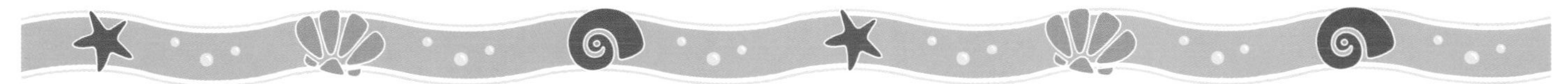

"You're too late," Ursula cried as she turned back into the monstrous sea witch. "She's my prisoner."

Ariel turned back into a mermaid. Ursula dragged her down to the very bottom of the sea.

Eric watched as they disappeared beneath the waves. "I can't lose her again," he said.

Ursula and Ariel went deeper and deeper.

"Ursula, stop," King Triton ordered. "Let her go."

Ursula smiled. "Ariel is mine," she said. "We had a deal. But I would be willing to exchange her for someone even better—like you."

King Triton did not have the power to break Ursula's spell. He loved his daughter too much and couldn't bear to see her as Ursula's prisoner, so he traded himself for Ariel's freedom.

Ursula put on King Triton's crown, and she used his powerful trident to become a gigantic and powerful ruler of the sea. Her head touched the clouds.

"I am the ruler of the entire ocean," Ursula cried. "Even the waves will obey me!"

Eric knew he had to save Ariel and destroy the sea witch. He managed to sail his boat right into Ursula, who sank to the bottom of the ocean and disappeared forever.

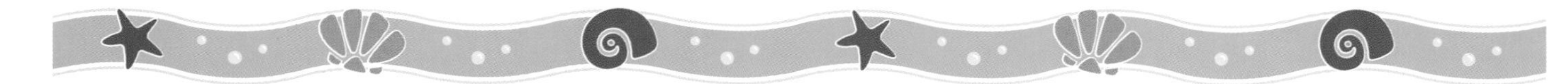

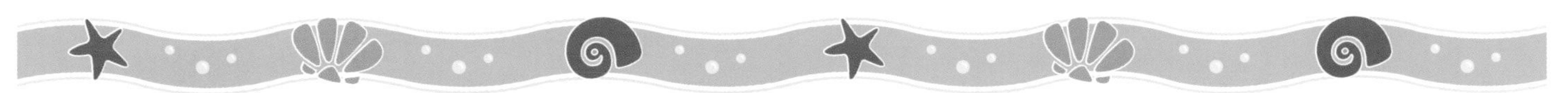

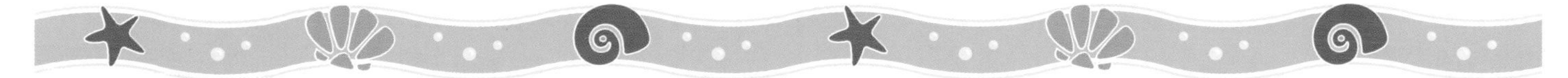

Eric had bravely saved the entire merworld. King Triton got his trident back, regained his powers, and was the kind ruler of the sea again.

King Triton and Sebastian went to talk to Ariel. They knew exactly where they would find her—above the sea, sitting on a rock watching Prince Eric. She wished with all her heart that they could be together.

King Triton watched his beautiful daughter. "She really loves him," he said to Sebastian. "I guess there's just one problem left," King Triton said.

"What's that, Your Majesty? " Sebastian asked.

"How much I'm going to miss her," King Triton exclaimed.

Then he waved his magic trident. Sparkles shot across the water and Ariel suddenly had two legs again.

It wasn't long before Prince Eric and Ariel were married. All of the mermen and mermaids came to the surface to see the royal wedding. King Triton was very proud. He knew his daughter had found a true prince.

DUMBO

Story adapted by Kate Hannigan

The circus was buzzing with excitement as a fleet of storks delivered babies for all of the animals. There was a joey for Mrs. Kangaroo, twin cubs for Mrs. Bear, and a baby hippo for Mrs. Hippopotamus. Only Mrs. Jumbo, the elephant, was sad. The stork didn't have a delivery for her.

The next morning, the circus train chugged down the tracks. It was springtime, and the animals were heading north after a winter break to perform for children everywhere.

High in the sky above them, a stork circled with a heavy bundle. "Mrs. Jumbo!" he called. "I have a delivery for you!"

The mother elephant was thrilled as the stork dropped off her baby. She peeked inside the blanket and fell in love. She decided to name her baby Jumbo Junior.

The other elephants gathered around to see the youngster. Mrs. Jumbo smiled proudly and tickled her baby under his chin with her long trunk.

Ah-choo! As Jumbo Junior sneezed, his ears flapped open. They were absolutely enormous!

The other elephants gasped. They pointed at Jumbo's huge ears and whispered. Then they began to laugh.

Mrs. Jumbo became angry at the other elephants. With her long trunk, she cradled Baby Jumbo.

"Jumbo?" said an elephant. "You mean Dumbo!"

The elephants laughed at the new name, but Mrs. Jumbo didn't care. She snuggled in the hay with her baby. She loved Dumbo, ears and all.

The next day was the circus show. Dumbo smiled happily at the crowds and waved his big ears. Some noisy children began to point at Dumbo and laugh. One boy reached over and tugged on his ears.

Mrs. Jumbo picked the boy up with her trunk and spanked him. The Ringmaster thought Mrs. Jumbo had gone crazy, so he locked her up.

Dumbo was sad. The other elephants turned their backs on him. He was all alone in the world, except for a little mouse named Timothy.

Timothy Mouse liked Dumbo and his big ears. Timothy told his friend to ignore the elephants. He thought Dumbo could be a star someday, so he helped him practice for a special circus act.

Dumbo had to jump to the top of an elephant pyramid! He practiced for hours, but he kept tripping on his big ears.

Timothy tied them in a knot on the top of Dumbo's head. "That ought to do the trick," he said.

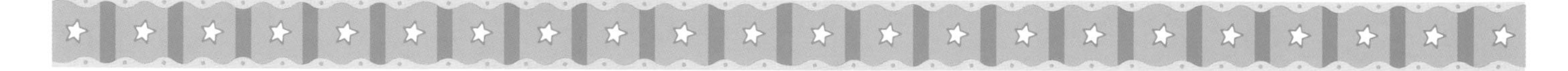

Trumpets blared and the curtain opened. It was Dumbo's big moment! He raced down the red carpet as Timothy cheered him on. But Dumbo's big ears came untied, and he tripped. He tumbled right into the pyramid!

The giant animals came crashing down, bringing the whole circus tent with them. It was a disaster!

The Ringmaster was so angry with Dumbo that he decided to make him perform with the clowns. The other circus elephants were humiliated. "From now on, Dumbo is no longer an elephant," they said.

Dumbo hated performing with the clowns. They threw water on him and made him jump from a tower into a tiny bucket. Dumbo was lonely and miserable.

Timothy Mouse felt sorry for Dumbo, so he arranged for Dumbo to see his mother. That made Dumbo happy again. He wanted to make her proud.

Dumbo went to sleep that night and had a wonderful dream. He dreamed he could fly—and it seemed so real!

Dumbo and Timothy woke in the morning to the sounds of birds chattering nearby. The birds were sitting on branches high in a tree—and so were Dumbo and Timothy Mouse! How in the world did they get there?

Timothy and Dumbo were so surprised to be up in the tree, they fell right out. The birds laughed as the friends splashed into the pond below.

Timothy wondered how they had gotten into the tree. The birds suggested that maybe Dumbo flew into the tree. Timothy felt that was possible. “Dumbo, just look at your ears!” he said. “They’re like wings.”

Timothy Mouse and the birds huddled together and tried to think of a way to make Dumbo fly again. Finally, the birds handed Timothy a black feather. Tell Dumbo it’s a magic feather, they said.

Dumbo perched on the edge of a high cliff. Timothy told Dumbo to hold the magic feather in his trunk and flap his ears.

Dumbo flapped and flapped, stirring up a cloud of dirt. When Dumbo opened his eyes, he was flying with the birds high above the treetops! Timothy Mouse was riding in Dumbo’s hat and cheering for his big friend.

When Dumbo and Timothy returned to the circus that night, they kept Dumbo’s new talent a secret. He prepared for his routine with the clowns just as he always did. Only this time, the clowns had raised Dumbo’s tower. It was so high, Dumbo could barely see the ground.

Trumpets blared, and the spotlight settled on Dumbo. He bravely stood at the edge of the tall tower, grasping his magic feather tightly in his trunk. It was his big moment.

Timothy Mouse gave Dumbo a smile and climbed into his hat. The friends were ready.

Dumbo jumped, and down, down, down they dropped. Suddenly the magic feather slipped from Dumbo's grasp! What were they going to do?

Timothy shouted into Dumbo's ear. He told him the feather wasn't really magic.

"You can fly all by yourself, Dumbo," Timothy yelled. "You can do it!"

At the last second, Dumbo flapped his enormous ears. He swooped over the crowd and flew around the circus tent. He glided gracefully through the air. He could do it! Dumbo could fly. The feather wasn't really magic after all.

Everyone in the audience jumped to their feet and cheered for Dumbo. They were amazed! They went home and told their friends. They came to the circus, too.

The Ringmaster was so happy, he brought Dumbo's mother back to live with Dumbo. Mrs. Jumbo couldn't believe her eyes. Her baby elephant could fly just like a bird!

Newspapers across the country ran stories about the flying elephant and his amazing, enormous ears. Word spread around the world. In every language, people talked about Dumbo's Flying Circus.

Mrs. Jumbo was proud of her son. She remembered the day he was delivered. She had always known her baby elephant was special. Now the rest of the world did, too.

The Ringmaster added a special railcar to the circus train for Dumbo and his mother. He wanted them to be comfortable since the circus had so many new towns and cities to visit.

From then on, Dumbo and his mother were always together. Whenever the circus train chugged along down the tracks, they could be seen laughing and playing in the last car.

Mrs. Jumbo would wrap Dumbo in a big hug with her long trunk. And Dumbo would smile happily as his enormous ears flapped in the breeze.

Pinocchio

Story adapted by Gayla Amaral

Long ago, a woodcarver named Geppetto lived in a beautiful cottage with his cat, Figaro, and his fish, Cleo. One night, Jiminy Cricket chanced upon the cottage. As the cricket entered and made himself comfortable, he watched Geppetto apply a final coat of paint to his latest project. It was a puppet with strings.

"I have just the name for you," said the woodcarver, maneuvering the strings to make his puppet dance around. "Pinocchio!"

Gazing out the window, Geppetto cried, "Look! It's the wishing star!" He whispered his heart's desire: "I wish that Pinocchio might be a real boy!"

As Geppetto drifted off to sleep, Jiminy was startled by a bright, shimmering light.

"It's a fairy!" he exclaimed.

The Blue Fairy said softly, "Dear Geppetto, you have given so much happiness to others. You deserve to have your wish come true."

She then touched Pinocchio with the tip of her wand, as she said, "Little puppet made of wood, awake!"

Pinocchio slowly began to move. "I can move! I can talk! I can walk!" he exclaimed. "Am I a real boy?"

The Fairy explained that one day he could be a real boy, but he must prove himself brave, truthful, and unselfish—and he must learn to choose between right and wrong. As Jiminy Cricket listened, she turned to him and asked, "Would you like to be Pinocchio's conscience?"

The cricket nodded, and the Fairy touched him with her wand. "I dub you Pinocchio's conscience—a guide along the straight and narrow path."

The Fairy's parting words were simple. "Be a good boy, Pinocchio," she said, "and always let your conscience be your guide."

But Pinocchio wasn't quite sure how a conscience worked. "How will I know right from wrong?" Pinocchio asked.

Jiminy tried to explain. He finally said, "Any time you need me, just whistle."

With all the commotion, it wasn't long before Geppetto awoke. "It's my wish! It's come true! This calls for a celebration!"

Now that Pinocchio was alive, Gepetto thought he should do the same things as real boys, like go to school. Pinocchio was excited about his first day of school. But on the way, he was spotted by a couple of greedy, crooked characters—a sly fox named Honest John and his crony, Gideon.

"A live puppet without strings!" exclaimed Honest John. "We can make a fortune selling him to the great Stromboli for his marionette show!"

Tempted by fame, Pinocchio was easily convinced to go with them. But he soon found himself locked in a cage, working for the evil Stromboli.

"Let me out!" Pinocchio shouted, shaking the cage. "Jiminy Cricket, help!" Jiminy tried, but he could not unlock the cage. Things were looking hopeless until the Blue Fairy appeared. When she questioned Pinocchio about what had happened, he told one lie after another.

"Two monsters with green eyes got me!" Pinocchio said. No sooner had he spoken when his nose began to grow.

"And they put me in a sack," he added. His nose continued to grow longer and longer. "My nose! What's happening?" he asked.

"A lie keeps growing and growing until it's as plain as the nose on your face," explained the Fairy.

"I'll never lie again. Please give me another chance," begged Pinocchio.

The good fairy agreed but warned him it would be his last chance.

Meanwhile, Geppetto searched everywhere for Pinocchio. He walked the streets calling out Pinocchio's name, but it was no use. He couldn't find his son anywhere.

Honest John and Gideon bragged to a wicked Coachman about selling Pinocchio to the puppeteer. They soon discovered that the Coachman had plans of his own. He tricked little boys who played hooky from school and took them to a place called Pleasure Island. The catch was that they never came back. The boys that went there turned into donkeys. Then they were sent off to work in the mines. The Coachman asked Honest John to bring him more boys.

Later that night, Honest John and Gideon just happened to cross paths with Pinocchio again. They were able to convince him to travel to Pleasure Island. As Pinocchio's conscience, Jiminy Cricket tried to stop Pinocchio from going. But the wooden boy wouldn't listen. Instead, he set sail for Pleasure Island.

Pinocchio and the other boys were thrilled to find a carnival with all the fun and food they could want. But things started to go bad when the boys began to turn into donkeys. Jiminy Cricket begged Pinocchio to leave, but it was too late. Pinocchio had already grown ears and a tail. What on earth was he going to do? If he didn't escape, he would be sent to work in the mines like the others.

"Jiminy, help!" Pinocchio cried when he spotted the cricket.

"Come quickly!" said Jiminy, leading him away from the island. "Jump into the water. It's the only way out!"

After crawling onto shore, Pinocchio and Jiminy hurried home, but Geppetto wasn't there. They did find a mysterious message informing them that Geppetto had gone to search for Pinocchio. According to the note, Geppetto had been swallowed by an enormous whale named Monstro.

Jiminy Cricket had heard of Monstro. He was a whale of a whale and had been known to swallow whole ships. But Pinocchio became brave and wasn't frightened at the thought of a whale. He ran straight to the ocean, tied a weight around his leg, and jumped in. He sank straight to the bottom.

Pinocchio was amazed at the schools of fish, but every time he asked them if they had seen Monstro the whale, they swam away as fast as they could. Just hearing the name of the great whale scared them off.

Meanwhile, Geppetto sat hopelessly inside the belly of the whale, desperately trying to catch fish for dinner. He thought he would never catch a thing until the big whale began to swim and eat, swallowing every fish in sight. Geppetto and Cleo reeled in fish after fish as fast the whale could swallow. But fish weren't the only things they reeled in. Pinocchio also ended up in the belly of the whale. He had found Geppetto!

Geppetto was delighted to see his little living puppet. They hugged and hugged! But in spite of his happiness, Geppetto told Pinocchio that their situation was hopeless and that they would never be able to escape. Just then, Pinocchio announced that he had an idea.

"We'll make Monstro sneeze!" suggested Pinocchio. So they gathered all the wood they could find and built a gigantic, roaring fire. Smoke filled the belly of the whale and escaped through his blowhole.

Sniff, sniff. The smoke was getting to Monstro. Geppetto and his family boarded their raft and waited for just the right moment. *Ah-ah-choo!*

"Hooray, we made it!" shouted the happy group as they sailed out of the whale's mouth and into the open sea.

Monstro was furious and began to swim after them.

"Hang on, Father," yelled Pinocchio as they were tossed about by the waves.

"Save yourself," Geppetto shouted to his son. Pinocchio wouldn't leave his father. When everyone made it safely to shore, they spotted Pinocchio lying very still.

Back home, Geppetto knelt beside the lifeless Pinocchio and cried, "My brave little boy!"

Cleo, Figaro, and Jiminy Cricket all cried as well. No one noticed a soft light shining on Pinocchio or heard the voice of the Blue Fairy softly saying, "Prove yourself brave, truthful, and unselfish, and someday you'll be a real boy. Awake, Pinocchio, awake!"

Pinocchio sat up. He was no longer a wooden puppet, but a real boy! "Father! Father! I'm alive! I'm a real boy!" he exclaimed.

Geppetto could hardly believe his eyes. It was true! Pinocchio had become a real boy at last.

"This calls for a celebration!" cried Geppetto. "Let the music begin!" Everyone danced happily as they celebrated the miraculous turn of events. Geppetto and Pinocchio lived happily ever after as father and son.

Treasure Planet

Story adapted by Lisa Harkrader

Jim Hawkins loved riding on his solar surfer. He also loved pirate stories, especially tales of Captain Flint. Flint had looted spaceships throughout the galaxy. He hid his treasure on Treasure Planet. Jim's mother said Treasure Planet was just a made-up story, but Jim knew the story was true. He vowed that one day he would find Treasure Planet for himself.

Jim's mother owned the Benbow Inn. One day an alien named Billy Bones crashed his ship outside the inn. He told Jim that pirates were chasing him. Billy Bones then gave Jim a small, odd-looking metal sphere.

"Beware of the cyborg," he whispered with his last breath.

"Cyborg?" said Jim. He knew that a cyborg was a creature that is part human and part machine.

As he tried to figure out what Billy Bones had meant, pirates attacked the inn. Jim, his mother, and their friend Dr. Doppler managed to escape, but the pirates burned the Benbow Inn to the ground.

Jim and his mother stayed at Doppler's house. Jim twirled the strange metal sphere in his hands. He unlocked the sphere and twisted it apart. Patterned lights beamed from inside the sphere and illuminated the room.

Jim studied the light beams. "It's a map!" he said.

Doppler pointed out their home planet on the map. But Jim found something even more interesting—Treasure Planet!

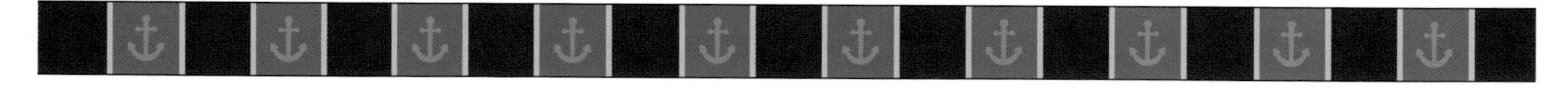

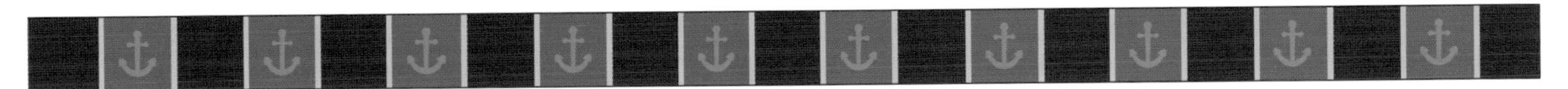

"I can use this to find Treasure Planet," said Jim.

"No," said his mother. "It's too dangerous."

"But if I find the treasure, we can rebuild the Benbow Inn," said Jim.

"He's right," said Doppler. "And I'll go with him."

Doppler hired a ship called the RLS *Legacy* to take them on their journey. Amelia, the ship's captain, locked the map securely in a chest in her stateroom.

"Don't speak of the treasure in front of the ship's crew," she told Jim and Doppler. "I don't trust them."

Captain Amelia told Jim that he would be working for the ship's cook during the journey. She sent Jim to the galley to meet the cook, John Silver.

"Pleased to meet you, Jimbo," said Silver.

When the cook reached out to shake Jim's hand, Jim saw that his metal arm was filled with gears and gadgets. One of his eyes wasn't an eye at all. It was a laser. Jim remembered what Billy Bones had told him: Beware of the cyborg. And John Silver was a cyborg!

The RLS *Legacy* set sail for Treasure Planet.

"Full speed," Captain Amelia ordered. "Brace yourselves!"

The ship shot through space. But Jim didn't have time to watch the sights go by. Silver kept him busy with many chores. Jim was scrubbing the deck and peeling potatoes.

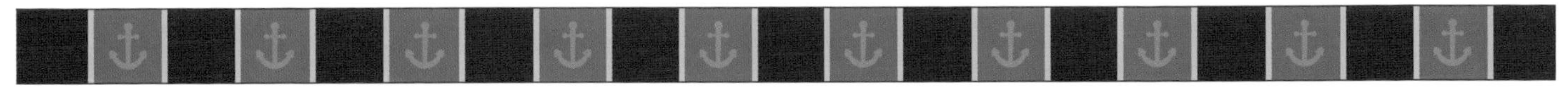

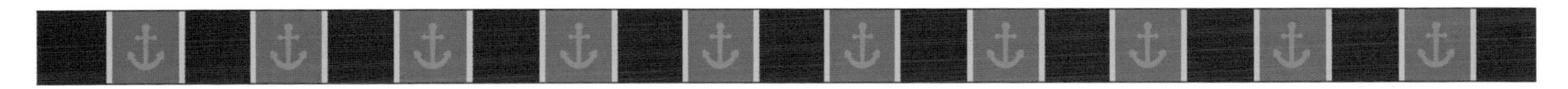

The crew onboard the *Legacy* didn't seem to like Jim very much. They would gang up on him and try to scare him, but Silver protected him. He knew Jim grew up without a father. Silver showed Jim how to tie knots and how to live onboard a ship. He let Jim pilot the ship's longboat. Even though Silver was a cyborg, Jim began to trust him.

But one day Jim overheard Silver talking to the crew in the galley. They were planning a mutiny.

"We want to take over the ship now," said one crewmember.

"No," said Silver. He was getting increasingly angry at the crew. "I'm giving the orders, and I say we don't move until we have the treasure map."

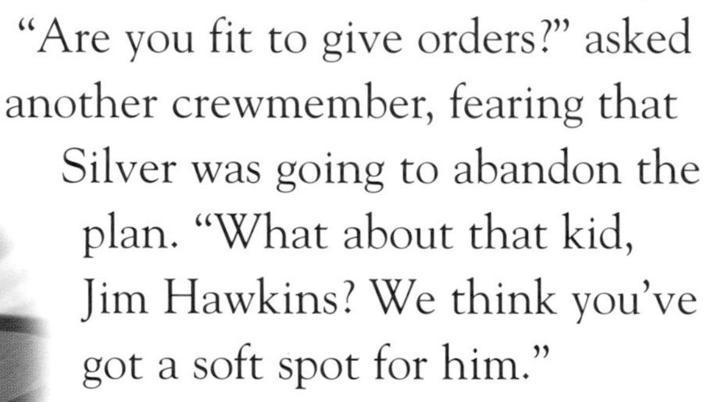

"Are you fit to give orders?" asked another crewmember, fearing that Silver was going to abandon the plan. "What about that kid, Jim Hawkins? We think you've got a soft spot for him."

"I care about one thing," said Silver angrily, "Flint's treasure. I cozied up to that kid to keep him off our scent. But I ain't gone soft."

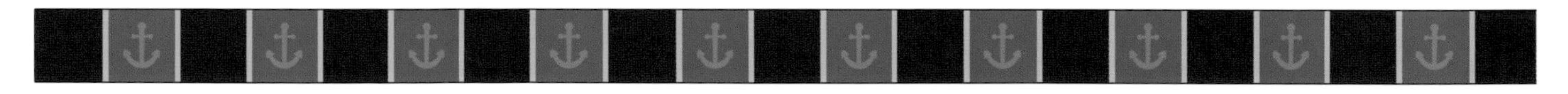

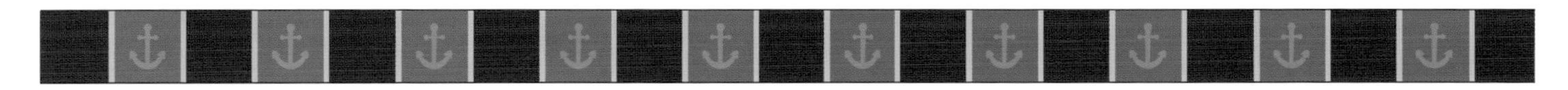

"Land ho!" the ship's lookout cried with excitement from the crow's nest. "Treasure Planet ahead."

The crew rushed on deck. Jim scurried from the galley, but Silver saw him. He knew Jim had been listening.

"Attack!" Silver called to the crew.

The crew overran the ship while Silver raised the pirate flag. Jim, Doppler, and Captain Amelia scrambled into the captain's stateroom and bolted the door. Captain Amelia unlocked the chest and tossed the map over to Jim.

"Defend this with your life," she said. "To the longboats. Quickly!"

The captain, Jim, and Doppler raced through the bowels of the ship, fighting off pirates. They reached one of the longboats, climbed aboard, and sailed off. But the pirates were right behind. They blasted the longboat with a laser ball. Captain Amelia tried to keep the boat sailing, but the shattered vessel crashed onto Treasure Planet. Luckily, no one was badly hurt, although Amelia's leg was slightly injured.

Jim, Doppler, and Amelia dusted themselves off. Jim reached for the map, but it was gone. "I must have left it on the ship!" he cried.

Captain Amelia sent Jim to scout out a better hiding place. He hadn't gone far when a metal figure leaped out. It was a robot.

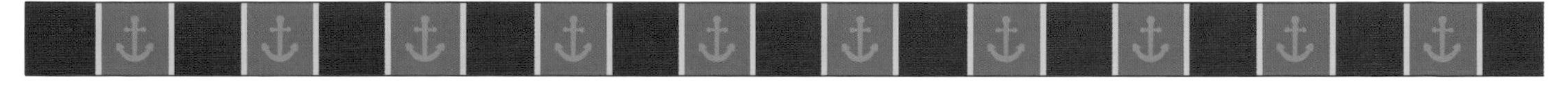

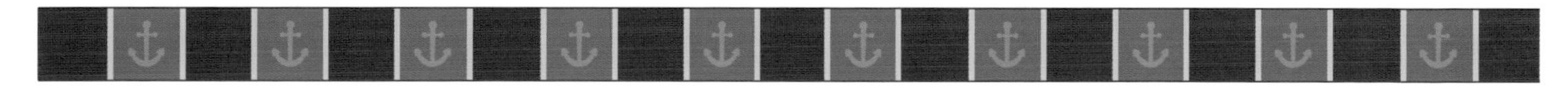

The robot hugged Jim. "A carbon-based life form come to rescue me at last! I've been stranded here for a hundred years. My name is B.E.N. That's short for Bio-Electronic Navigator."

"I'm Jim," said Jim. "I'm trying to find a place to hide from pirates."

"I know about pirates!" said B.E.N. "I remember Captain Flint. He was so mean—"

"You knew Captain Flint?" interrupted Jim. "Then you must know where the treasure is."

"Treasure?" B.E.N. thumped his metal head. "Oh, yes, I remember the treasure. I helped Captain Flint hide it. But I don't remember where."

B.E.N. took Jim, Doppler, and Captain Amelia to the cave where he lived. They'd barely settled in before the pirates found them. The pirates surrounded the cave and waited for Jim and the others to come out.

But B.E.N. showed Jim a secret passage in the back of the cave. When night fell, Jim and B.E.N sneaked out the back passage. They borrowed a pirate's longboat and slipped aboard the *Legacy*. Jim found the map. He and B.E.N. returned to the planet and slipped back into the cave.

"I've got it!" said Jim.

Silver stepped from the shadows. "Fine work, Jimbo."

Jim realized they were in trouble. He was grabbed by the pirates.

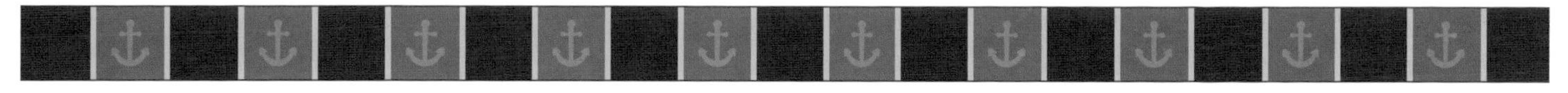

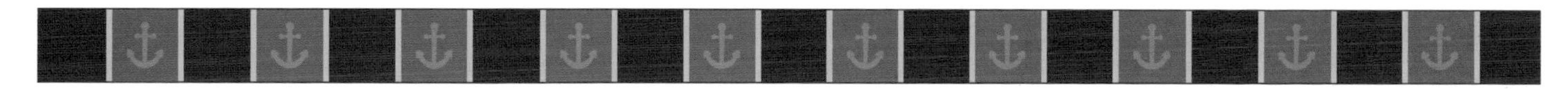

The pirates had tied up Doppler and Amelia. They forced Jim to use his knowledge of the map to take them to the treasure. Jim opened the portal to the planet's core. The core was filled with gold coins and jewels, with Captain Flint's ship perched in the center.

Silver dropped to his knees. "I've found it at last!" he exclaimed.

The planet began to quake. "I remember now," said B.E.N. "Flint rigged the entire planet to blow up if anybody found his treasure."

Suddenly, the ground split beneath their feet. Jim and B.E.N. leaped aboard Captain Flint's ship. Jim fixed the wiring and fired up the ship.

"Not so fast." Silver leaped aboard. "This ship's filled with treasure, and I'm taking it."

Just then, an explosion rocked the ship. Jim plunged overboard. He began sliding into a huge crater. Silver had to choose between saving Jim and saving the treasure. He pulled Jim to safety.

Captain Amelia had already fired up the *Legacy*. Jim, B.E.N., and Silver scrambled aboard.

"We have exactly two minutes and thirty-four seconds until the planet's complete destruction," said B.E.N.

"Turn back," Jim said. "I can save us."

Doppler steered the ship back. Jim used a makeshift solar surfer and some fancy moves to reach the portal map. He touched the map, opening a portal door right in front of them. Dopler steered the ship through.

Once safe, Silver knew he must leave the ship or face jail. He tossed Jim a handful of gold coins from his pocket. "For your dear mother," he said, "to rebuild that inn of hers." He leaped onto a longboat and waved as he sailed away.

Jim's mother did rebuild the Benbow Inn, and B.E.N. became her cook. Doppler and Captain Amelia were to be wed. And Jim became the captain of his own ship. Everyone lived happily ever after.

Story adapted by Lynne Roberts

The London docks buzzed with excitement. John Smith and his crew were ready to set sail for new land. They were looking for gold. John Smith was very strong and brave. He had been on many trips to see new and wonderful places.

Across the ocean, a young woman named Pocahontas was playing with her friend, Nakoma. Pocahontas was not afraid to explore on her own or dive from tall cliffs into the water. Nakoma was always telling Pocahontas to be careful.

"You worry too much," said Pocahontas.

"You don't worry enough," replied Nakoma as she watched her friend.

Pocahontas just laughed. She swam under Nakoma's canoe and tipped it over. The two friends laughed and played in the water.

Pocahontas and Nakoma belonged to the same tribe. They believed that the earth was special and each animal and plant had its own spirit.

Pocahontas liked to explore the forest with her raccoon friend, Meeko, and her hummingbird friend, Flit. Meeko and Flit were not as brave as Pocahontas, but they enjoyed her adventures. They especially liked to visit Grandmother Willow. Grandmother Willow was a wise old tree who spoke to Pocahontas and helped her discover the answers to life's questions.

Pocahontas told Grandmother Willow about a dream she had. In her dream, Pocahontas saw strange clouds and a spinning arrow. She felt the arrow was pointing her to the right path in her life. Pocahontas said that she also felt something exciting was coming to her land. She knew that whatever it was would change her life forever. Grandmother Willow told Pocahontas to listen to her heart and to listen to the wind.

Then one day Pocahontas saw the strange clouds from her dream floating above some trees. She had not understood that what she saw in her dream were not clouds, but the large white sails of a ship.

The ship was John Smith's. He and the other English settlers had arrived at the new land. Governor Ratcliffe claimed the land for England and King James. He called this new land "Jamestown." He did not care if other people already lived on the land; he felt it belonged to England. The settlers were very excited about their search for gold. Each man grabbed a shovel and began to dig right away.

Pocahontas was curious about the strange clouds she had seen. She got in her canoe and went to explore. At the river bend, she saw something curious. It looked like a man, but not like any man she had ever seen. This man had light hair and strange clothing. He spoke to Pocahontas, but she did not understand his words. She then remembered the words of Grandmother Willow. She had told Pocahontas to listen to the wind. A breeze blew leaves around John Smith and the sound of his voice. Suddenly, Pocahontas understood this man's language. She spoke back. "I'm Pocahontas," she said.

John Smith took her hand. He was enchanted by this beautiful girl. He had never seen anyone who looked like Pocahontas.

On the shore near the ship, the settlers were digging up the land. They could not find any gold. The settlers were also being watched by men from Pocahontas's tribe. They wondered what the strangers were doing. Their behavior was so odd, it made the tribesmen uneasy.

John Smith and Pocahontas spent the day together. Pocahontas taught John Smith how her people loved the earth. She told him how every rock, tree, and living creature has a spirit. For futher proof, she took him to meet Grandmother Willow. John Smith was amazed! He had never seen a talking tree. Especially one that told jokes.

"My bark is worse than my bite," said Grandmother Willow, laughing.

Just then, Meeko brought Pocahontas a compass that he had taken from John Smith. That was a sign. Pocahontas knew that John Smith was the reason for her strange dream. She realized that the arrow on the compass was the arrow in her dream. She watched the arrow spin and spin, only to stop while pointing at John Smith. With the help of Grandmother Willow's advice, Pocahontas knew that John Smith was her true love, her right path.

As Pocahontas and John Smith shared a special moment together, they were spotted by others in her tribe. The tribesmen misunderstood and thought that John Smith was trying to hurt Pocahontas. The men attacked John Smith and captured him. They took him to see their leader, Pocahontas's father, Chief Powhatan.

Chief Powhatan felt threatened having this stranger on his land. He did not understand that John Smith was in love with his daughter. He decided that John Smith would be dealt with at sunrise.

During the night, the English sailors had learned that John Smith was being held captive by the natives of this new land. They discussed what should be done. The men thought the tribesmen were dangerous. The English settlers decided they had to fight them.

As of yet, the settlers had not uncovered any gold. They felt that if these dangerous people were gone, then they could claim the land and the gold for their own. The settlers prepared for battle.

As the sun rose the next day, John Smith was led to the tip of a rock that overlooked the land. Chief Powhatan wanted to punish John Smith. He felt that this would scare away the other strangers as well.

Just as they reached the rock, the English settlers appeared. They were ready to attack. The men of the tribe stood armed and ready to defend themselves and their land.

Pocahontas felt that the fighting was not necessary. She knew the two tribes could learn from one another. She threw herself in front of John Smith and begged that the fighting be stopped.

Chief Powhatan looked at his daughter. He suddenly understood that she loved John Smith. Chief Powhatan put his hand up to stop the battle. Everyone saw this as a gesture of peace. They all put down their weapons. The battle was over before it even began.

The settlers wanted to make peace. They could see that Pocahontas and Chief Powhatan were kind. They saw that the tribe did not want to fight. But evil Governor Ratcliffe did not care. He wanted to fight anyway and ordered the settlers to fire their guns. The Englishmen refused. Governor Ratcliffe decided that he would do it himself and took aim at Chief Powhatan.

John Smith anticipated Ratcliffe's decision and pushed the chief out of the way. The chief was safe, but John Smith had been hurt badly. The medicine man in the village could not heal John Smith. Everyone knew that John Smith had to get back to England. He needed to be in the care of a doctor. Chief Powhatan gave John Smith a special blanket to keep him warm. Pocahontas comforted him while they waited for the preparations to be made. She told him that everything would be all right. John Smith knew that Pocahontas was right.

The people from the village brought food for the settlers' journey back to England. They had corn, wheat for bread, and other fruits and vegetables. The Englishmen were grateful for the supplies.

Chief Powhatan told John Smith that he was always welcome among his people. John Smith thanked the Chief. He hoped to come back one day and it felt good to know that he would be warmly welcomed.

The time came for the English ship to set sail for London. John Smith asked Pocahontas to come with him. She told him that she must stay with her people. She was needed for her wisdom and kindness. Even though he would miss her terribly, John Smith understood.

"I will always be with you, Pocahontas," said John Smith.

"And my spirit will always be with you, John Smith," said Pocahontas.

She hoped that she would see John Smith again, but she knew it would be a long time before they could be together. Despite her sadness, Pocahontas remained brave.

An English sailor rowed John Smith to the ship. John Smith was very sad. He knew that Pocahontas was special. Someday, he hoped, he would come back to the beautiful New World and see Pocahontas again.

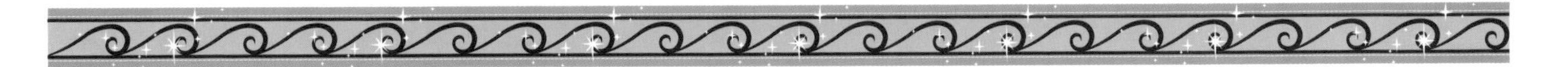

Cinderella

Story adapted by Kate Hannigan

Once upon a time in a faraway land, there lived a beautiful young girl named Cinderella.

Cinderella was loving and kind, and she was adored by everyone—everyone, that is, except her cruel stepmother and two mean stepsisters. They treated Cinderella like a servant.

"Clean the kitchen," said one stepsister.

"Fix the breakfast," ordered the other.

"Bring me my tea!" shouted the Stepmother.

Cinderella never had a moment to herself. She filled the teapots, grabbed the teacups, and scooped up the trays. Balancing everything on her hands and head, she hurried up the stairs.

Lucifer the cat chased after Cinderella. He was always up to no good, and this morning was no different. He had caught a mouse and hidden it under one of the teacups. But which one?

"Eek!" shrieked Anastasia. "A mouse!" She ran out of her room in her nightdress, pointing at Cinderella. Anastasia and Drizella thought Cinderella had put the mouse there.

Cinderella's Stepmother was angry and called Cinderella into her dark room. "You have time for practical jokes?" she asked. "Maybe you need more work to do."

The Stepmother gave Cinderella more chores than ever.

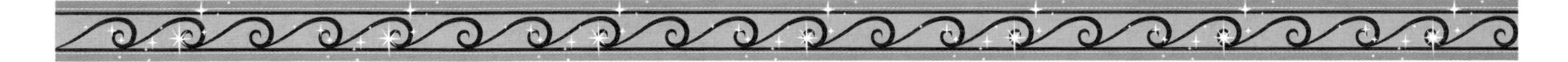

Cinderella was scrubbing the floors when she heard a knock at the door. A messenger for the King delivered an invitation. Every maiden in the kingdom was to come to the Prince's ball!

Cinderella ran to her room. In an old trunk she found a pink dress that had belonged to her mother. If she added ribbon and changed the sleeves, she thought, it would be perfect.

The stepsisters kept Cinderella so busy, she had no time to fix her dress.

Inside her room, Cinderella's friends, the mice and birds, had a surprise for her. They had fixed her mother's old dress! Cinderella thanked them and hugged the gown. Now she could go to the ball!

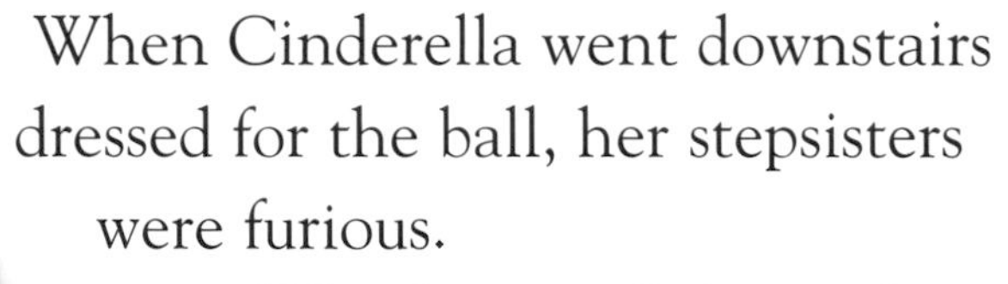

When Cinderella went downstairs dressed for the ball, her stepsisters were furious.

"That's mine!" shouted Anastasia, tugging on Cinderella's bead necklace. "And that's mine," said Drizella, tearing off a sash.

Before she could stop them, the stepsisters had ruined Cinderella's new dress.

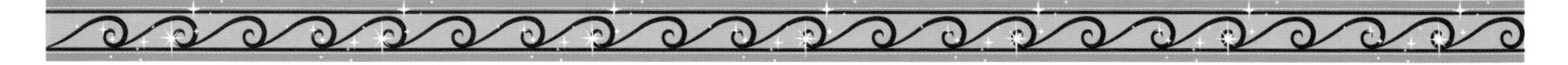

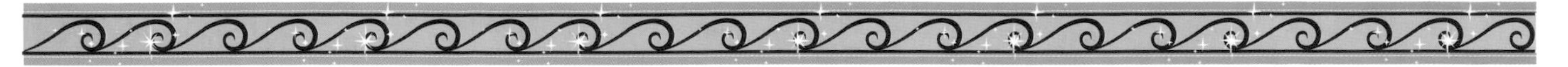

Cinderella ran to the garden, crying. She wanted to see the royal palace and meet the Prince. "But that will never happen now," she sobbed.

"It's not hopeless," said a voice. "Dry your eyes, my child."

Cinderella looked up. There sat her Fairy Godmother, surrounded by a swirl of sparkles like magical fireflies.

The Fairy Godmother waved her magic wand and turned a bright orange pumpkin into a delicate coach. Then she spotted Cinderella's friends, the mice, and waved her wand again. Poof! She turned them into four white horses. "Now you're ready for the ball!" she said.

Cinderella didn't want to seem ungrateful, but she needed a gown to wear, too. The Fairy Godmother looked at her tattered dress and agreed.

"Oh, my! You can't go in that!" With a wave of her wand, the Fairy Godmother transformed Cinderella's rags into a beautiful gown with sparkly glass slippers.

She told Cinderella to enjoy the ball. "But remember," she said, "the spell will be broken at midnight."

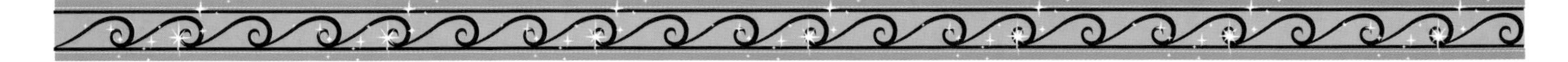

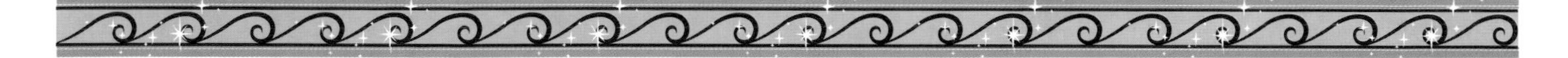

Cinderella arrived at the palace and climbed the sweeping staircase to the ballroom. Everyone's eyes turned toward the doorway and the beautiful girl standing there. "Who is she?" they asked.

The Prince took one look at Cinderella and fell in love. He held out his hands, and they danced the whole night.

Cinderella thought the Prince was handsome and kind, and she fell in love, too. She was having so much fun, she forgot about the time. She could have danced with him all night long.

Suddenly the clock struck midnight. Cinderella dashed toward the staircase. She had to get home!

"But wait," called the Prince. "I don't even know your name!"

Cinderella raced down the stairs. She was in such a hurry to get away, she left one of her glass slippers on the staircase.

She jumped into the coach, and the horses ran as fast as they could. As the clock sounded the twelfth toll—*poof!*—the coach turned back into a pumpkin. It bounced along the road as—*poof! poof!*—the horses turned back into mice, and Cinderella's gown turned back into her old rags.

Cinderella and her friends sat by the side of the road. The Prince's guards raced by on horseback, squashing the orange pumpkin.

All Cinderella had left of her magical night was the other glass slipper.

The Prince had to find the woman from the ball. He ordered the Grand Duke to search the kingdom for the girl whose foot fit the glass slipper. The Prince would marry that woman.

Cinderella's Stepmother heard the news and ran to tell her daughters. There was still a chance one of them could marry the Prince, she thought.

The Grand Duke arrived at Cinderella's house. Anastasia sat down and tried on the glass slipper. She tugged and pulled, but the slipper would not fit. She pinched and pushed, but the slipper would not fit.

"Let me try," said Drizella. She tugged and pulled and pinched and pushed. But the slipper would not fit her either.

As the Grand Duke turned to leave, he asked if there were any other ladies at home.

"No, just my daughters," answered the Stepmother. She had locked Cinderella in her room!

At the last moment, Cinderella's friends, the mice, slipped her the key. Cinderella unlocked the door and raced downstairs. But the Stepmother tripped the Duke. The slipper sailed through the air before finally shattering on the floor!

"It's all right," said Cinderella. "I have the other one right here."

Cinderella pulled the other glass slipper from her pocket and tried it on. It was a perfect fit!

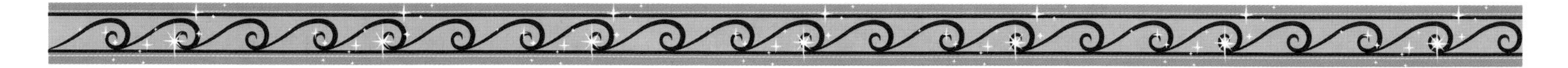

"It fits!" gasped the Stepmother.

"It fits!" shrieked the stepsisters.

"It fits!" sighed the Grand Duke.

Cinderella and the Grand Duke raced back to the castle. The Prince was overjoyed to see the maiden he'd fallen in love with. He proposed to Cinderella on the spot. She accepted and they were married that day.

Church bells rang throughout the kingdom for Cinderella and the Prince's wedding. Everyone cheered as they ran down the staircase. Cinderella was so excited, she didn't even notice she'd left something behind on the staircase. It was one of her glass wedding slippers!

Cinderella slipped it back on and jumped into the coach with the Prince. They waved good-bye to their friends, the mice. Cinderella was happy knowing that this time there was no magical spell to be broken.

Beauty and the Beast

Story adapted by Amy Adair

Once upon a time, there lived a young prince. The Prince was selfish and unkind. One night, he heard a heavy knock on his door. It was an old beggar woman. Before he could shut the door, the beggar offered him a single rose in exchange for a night of shelter.

The Prince laughed at the thought of the poor beggar staying in the castle. The old woman warned the Prince that true beauty is not always seen on the outside, but can be found inside a person as well.

Suddenly, the beggar became a beautiful enchantress. The Prince begged for forgiveness, but it was too late. The Enchantress had already seen the kind of person the Prince was, and she decided that he should be taught a proper lesson.

The Enchantress turned the prince into an ugly beast. Then she placed a powerful spell on the castle and all who lived there.

The rose she had offered was enchanted. It would continue to bloom until the Prince's twenty-first year. Petals would fall over the years, but if he could learn to love and be loved in return before the last petal fell, then the spell would be broken. If not, he would remain a beast forever.

As the years passed, the Beast fell into despair. He had lost all hope of ever breaking the spell, for who could ever learn to love a beast?

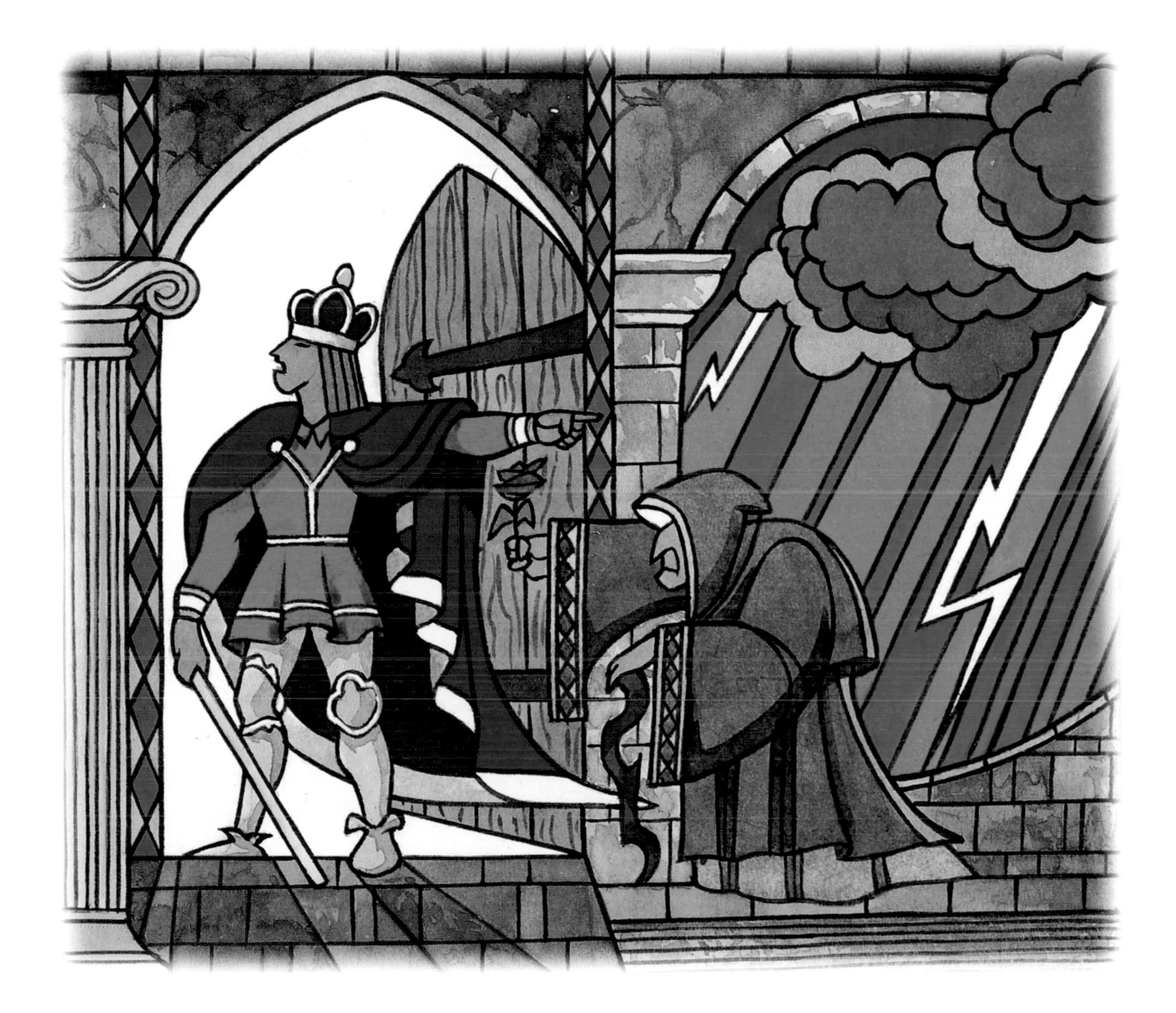

Belle lived in a quiet village with her Papa. Every day was exactly the same. Belle wasn't at all like the other villagers. They seemed happy in the small town. But Belle wanted to explore castles and far-off places.

One bright morning, Belle went to the bookstore to find her favorite book. It was about a prince. Belle couldn't wait to begin reading it again. She enjoyed stories about princes very much, especially stories in which an ordinary woman meets a handsome prince and they fall in love. She turned to her favorite part of the book and read as she walked.

Suddenly, Gaston jumped in front of her. Gaston thought Belle was the most beautiful girl in the entire village. He was determined to make her his wife. All the other girls dreamed of becoming Gaston's wife. They thought he was tall, dark, and handsome. But Belle thought Gaston was rude.

"Hello, Belle," Gaston said, taking the book out of her hands. "There aren't any pictures in this book."

Belle shook her head and grabbed her book.

"I'm going to make you the happiest woman in the whole village," Gaston said. "I'm going to make you my wife."

Belle shook her head. She couldn't imagine spending her life as Gaston's wife.

"I have to hurry home," Belle said.

Belle's papa, Maurice, was going to a fair to show off his new invention. On the way, Maurice's horse, Phillipe, got scared and ran away. Maurice was alone in the dark forest. He wandered in the darkness until he found a castle.

Knock, knock! When no one answered, he pushed the door open.

Maurice walked past a candlestick and a clock. "Not a word, Lumiere," Cogsworth, the clock, said to the candlestick.

"Have a heart," Lumiere told Cogsworth. Then he turned to Maurice and said, "You're welcome here!"

At first Maurice was scared. He had never seen a talking candlestick or clock before. But he was thankful for their kindness. They went into a large room with a comfortable chair and a warm fireplace.

Maurice settled into the chair as the door opened. "Who are you?" roared the Beast. "You are not welcome here."

"I just need a place to stay," Maurice stuttered.

"I'll give you a place to stay," the Beast said, and he threw Maurice into a cold, dark dungeon.

It wasn't long before Phillipe found his way home. "Where's Papa?" Belle asked. "You must take me to him."

Phillipe led Belle through the forest to the Beast's castle. Belle held her breath and pounded on the castle door. When no one answered, she slowly pushed it open.

She wandered through the dark halls and finally found her papa. "Oh, Papa," Belle cried.

Belle heard a terrible roar. "Who's there?" she called out.

"I'm the master of this castle," the Beast replied.

"Please let my father come home with me," Belle begged. "He's sick."

"He's my prisoner," the Beast said.

"Will you let him go if I stay in his place?" Belle asked.

The Beast stepped into the light. Belle gasped when she saw him. "Will you promise to stay here forever?" the Beast asked.

Belle took a deep breath.

"Yes," she cried. With that, the Beast threw Maurice out before Belle could even say good-bye.

Everyone in the castle whispered about the beautiful stranger. Even the Beast hoped that she would be the one to finally break the spell.

The Beast took Belle to a comfortable room. "You can go anywhere you like," he said, "except the west wing. It's forbidden." When the Beast shut the door, Belle sat on the floor and cried. She was sure none of her dreams would ever come true now.

There was a soft knock on the door. "I thought you'd like a spot of tea," said a kind teapot named Mrs. Potts.

Later that night, Belle tiptoed down the stairs and found Mrs. Potts and Lumiere. They made her a feast fit for a princess.

Lumiere and Cogsworth showed her the rest of the castle. Belle snuck away to explore on her own. As she wandered the hallways, she went into the forbidden west wing. There she found a single red rose. It looked magical. Just as she was reaching out to touch it, the Beast yelled, "I warned you never to come here!"

Belle gasped. She couldn't stay in the castle with this horrible Beast. She flew down the steps and out the castle door.

It was dark and snowy. Suddenly, hungry wolves surrounded her. The Beast came to her rescue, but he was badly wounded. Belle took the Beast back to the castle.

Slowly, the castle started to feel like Belle's home. She liked all of her new friends, and she even started to care for the Beast.

Belle and the Beast spent every waking moment together. They talked for hours and even took long walks in the garden and fed the birds.

Belle didn't see an ugly Beast when she looked at him. Instead, when she looked into the Beast's blue eyes she saw kindness and love.

One night, the Beast planned a very special dinner. It was exactly what Belle had imagined in her dreams. They danced together just like a real prince and princess.

"Are you happy here with me?" the Beast asked.

Belle nodded. But then she remembered her father. She missed him. "I'd like to see my father again," Belle said sadly.

The Beast understood. He showed Belle his magic mirror. Inside the mirror, Belle saw her father. He was alone and very sick. Belle desperately wanted to be by his side.

The Beast looked at the rose. The last petal would fall soon. He knew that if Belle left the castle, the spell would never be broken. He'd remain a Beast forever. But he loved Belle, and he wanted her to be happy.

"You must go to him," he said quietly. The Beast gave Belle his magic mirror so that she would always remember him.

Belle returned home to her father. He was so happy to see her. She explained that the Beast was, in fact, very kind and gentle.

Gaston came by their house and saw the magic mirror the Beast had given Belle. He saw an image of the Beast in the mirror and gathered others from the village to go to the castle.

Gaston wanted to destroy the Beast. But the Beast would not fight. Then the Beast spotted Belle. He reached out for her hand, but Gaston wounded him. The Beast roared out in pain. Gaston lost his footing and fell.

Belle thought the Beast was gone forever. "Please don't leave me," she sobbed. "I love you."

Firecrackers burst over the castle. The Beast was transformed into a handsome prince. Belle saw that he still had the Beast's kind blue eyes.

Belle's love had broken the spell. She and the Prince were married and lived a long and happy life together.

THE JUNGLE BOOK

Story adapted by Lisa Harkrader

A strange sound broke the silence of the jungle. Bagheera the panther leaped through the trees, following the sound. Nestled in a basket on the banks of the stream, he found a Man-cub—a baby!

The baby needed a mother, but the nearest Man-village was far away. So Bagheera took the baby to a family of wolves, who named him Mowgli. They raised him as one of their own. Bagheera stayed nearby as the boy grew, and he became Mowgli's friend.

When Mowgli was ten, the wolf pack held a meeting. Shere Khan the tiger had returned to their part of the jungle. The wolves were worried about Mowgli. Shere Khan hated Man. Man made the one thing Shere Khan was afraid of: fire. The wolves knew that Shere Khan would attack Mowgli and any wolf who tried to protect the boy. They told Rama, Mowgli's wolf father, that Mowgli must leave the pack.

"But Mowgli can't survive alone in the jungle," said Rama.

Bagheera had been listening. "Perhaps I can help," he told the wolves. "I know of a Man-village where he'll be safe. I'll take him there."

Bagheera and Mowgli set off through the jungle.

Bagheera didn't tell Mowgli where they were going. Mowgli wouldn't go if he knew he had to leave the jungle. Mowgli thought he and Bagheera were going on an adventure.

That night they stopped to sleep in a tall tree. But while Bagheera dozed, Kaa the snake slithered toward Mowgli. He coiled his long snake body around Mowgli and opened his mouth wide to swallow him. But Bagheera awoke just in time to save the boy.

Kaa tried to hypnotize Bagheera, but Mowgli pushed him out of the tree. Kaa fell to the ground with a knot in his tail.

After a short nap, Bagheera and Mowgli were awakened by a parade of elephants. The leader was Colonel Hathi. He and the elephants patrolled the jungle to keep it safe. The Colonel saw Mowgli and was outraged.

"I'll have no Man-cub in my jungle!" the Colonel said.

"Don't worry," Bagheera said. "I'm taking Mowgli to the Man-village."

"Good," said Colonel Hathi as the elephants marched away.

"But I don't want to go to the Man-village," Mowgli told Bagheera. "I want to stay in the jungle."

"It's not safe for you here," said Bagheera. He could tell that Mowgli would be sad to leave.

After the two friends had an argument, Bagheera left Mowgli. Mowgli sat down to rest. Baloo the bear passed by. He stopped to sniff Mowgli.

"Go away," said Mowgli. He tried to fight off Baloo.

"You need help, kid," said Baloo. "I'll teach you to fight like a bear."

Baloo showed Mowgli how to growl like a bear, too. Bagheera heard the growls and came running back.

"Oh, it's just you, Baloo," said Bagheera. "Come, Mowgli. We have to get you to the Man-village."

"Man-village?" said Baloo. "They'll turn him into a man. You'll stay with me. I'll teach you everything you need to know."

Baloo taught Mowgli to find ants under rocks and to scratch his back on a tree. But when he taught Mowgli to float in the river, a troop of monkeys snatched Mowgli away. Before Baloo and Bagheera could stop them, the monkeys carried Mowgli off to their king in an ancient temple.

Baloo and Bagheera raced to the temple and rescued Mowgli.

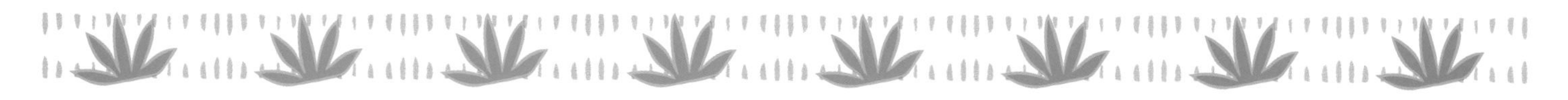

"You see?" Bagheera told Baloo. "Mowgli keeps getting into trouble. He can't live in the jungle. Shere Khan will find him, and you won't be able to protect him. Mowgli must go to the Man-village. And you must take him there. He'll listen to you. He doesn't listen to me."

Baloo nodded. "You're right," he said sadly.

But when Baloo tried to take Mowgli to the Man-village, Mowgli ran away. Baloo and Bagheera searched the jungle, but they couldn't find the boy anywhere.

Bagheera stopped the elephant patrol. "We need your help," he told Colonel Hathi. "The Man-cub is lost. We must find him."

Shere Khan was hunting nearby. He heard Bagheera. "Man-cub?" he said to himself. The thought of a delicious Man-cub made Shere Khan very hungry. He had to find the boy.

Colonel Hathi organized the elephants to search for Mowgli. Shere Khan set out on a search of his own. He stalked through the jungle looking for Mowgli.

Kaa the snake found Mowgli first. He coiled his body around Mowgli. Before he could harm the boy, Shere Khan passed by. Kaa hid Mowgli in his coils. After Kaa spoke to Shere Khan, Mowgli escaped. He pushed Kaa from the tree again, and then wandered off through the jungle once more.

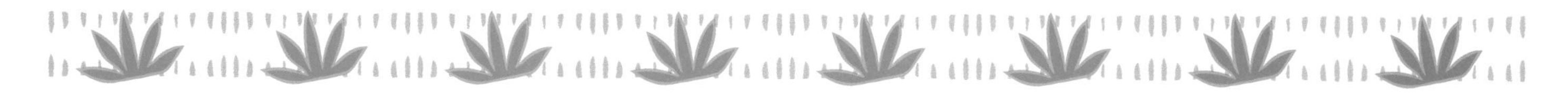

A storm was brewing over the jungle. Mowgli was tired and lost. He sat down to rest. A flock of vultures was roosting in a tree nearby. The vultures saw that Mowgli was alone. They swooped down from their tree.

"You can join our group," they told him.

Shere Khan heard the vultures talking to Mowgli. He raced from his hiding spot in the brush.

Shere Khan crouched down. But before he could pounce on Mowgli, Baloo leaped out and grabbed the tiger's tail.

"Run, Mowgli!" cried Baloo.

But Mowgli said he wasn't afraid, and he didn't run. When Shere Khan turned and attacked Baloo, Mowgli beat the tiger with a stick.

"Take that, you bully," said Mowgli.

Shere Khan turned to pounce on Mowgli, but the vultures swooped down and carried Mowgli from the tiger's claws.

As Mowgli, Baloo, and the vultures fought Shere Khan, thunder cracked overhead. Lightning struck the vultures' tree, setting it on fire.

"Fire!" cried the vultures. "It's the only thing Shere Khan is afraid of."

Mowgli picked up a flaming stick and waved it at Shere Khan. The tiger backed away in fear. He raced off into the jungle.

"We won't be seeing him around here again," said the vultures.

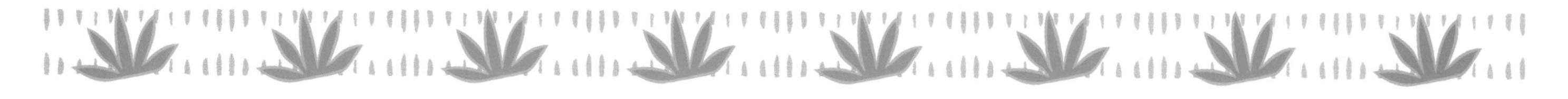

Bagheera heard the fighting. He raced through the jungle and found Mowgli safe. He, Baloo, and Mowgli set out once more for the Man-village.

Soon a strange sound broke the silence of the jungle. Mowgli leaped through the trees, following the sound. It was a girl. She was singing as she gathered water from a stream. She was the first human being Mowgli had ever seen. And she was beautiful.

The girl set off back through the jungle. Mowgli followed. When the girl dropped her jar of water, Mowgli filled it in the stream again. Then he carried the jar for her. He followed the girl all the way to her village.

"He's home now," said Bagheera. "Mowgli is in the Man-village. It's where he belongs."

Baloo nodded. "Too bad," he said. "That kid would have made one swell bear."

Story adapted by Gayla Amaral

Sometimes the smallest things make the biggest changes in the lives of others. That's exactly what happened 65 million years ago when a dinosaur egg containing an iguanodon was taken from the safety of its nest.

After Aladar's friends and family were attacked by a group of carnotaurs, the egg in which Aladar lived was miraculously transported over land, sea, and sky to a distant island. Landing in the midst of a lemur clan, the egg was the object of much attention. The curious Plio was the first to investigate.

"Dad, come look," called Plio to the older monkey. The egg was beginning to crack. She watched as the baby iguanodon entered the world.

"It's a cold-blooded monster," warned Yar, the elder lemur. "Things like that eat things like us for snacks!"

Plio didn't believe him for a minute. "Look at that sweet little face. Does that look like a monster to you?" she asked.

Yar couldn't resist the adorable Aladar. And that's how a dinosaur came to be raised by a clan of lemurs.

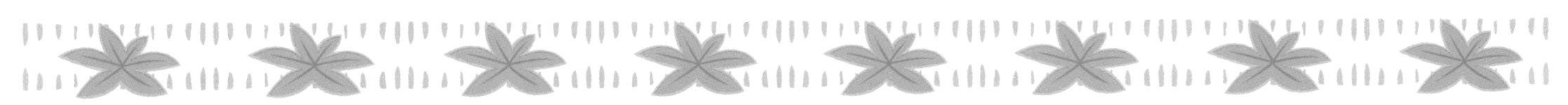

The sound of screaming and chittering could be heard throughout the forest. Aladar was chasing the young lemurs through the trees and was quickly gaining on them. But the screams were screams of delight as they laughed and played with their fun-loving dinosaur friend.

"Pick on someone your own size," Aladar groaned, pretending to be afraid, while Suri and the other lemurs jumped all over him. Aladar enjoyed pretending to be afraid of his little friends.

"Hurry up," said Plio as she interrupted their playtime. "You don't want to miss the annual courtship ritual."

As the little lemurs scampered away, Aladar set out to find his friend Zini, one of the eligible bachelors. Swinging from vines high in the Ritual Tree, everyone seemed to have found the perfect match. Everyone, that is, except poor Zini.

"Don't worry," said Aladar. "You'll find someone next year."

As Zini walked away, Plio gave Aladar a hug. Zini wasn't the only bachelor left in the clan. Aladar was a lone dinosaur in a family of lemurs. Plio longed for Aladar to meet someone of his kind as well.

"Oh, Aladar, if only there were someone on the island for you," she sighed.

"Come on, Plio," responded Aladar. "What more could I want?"

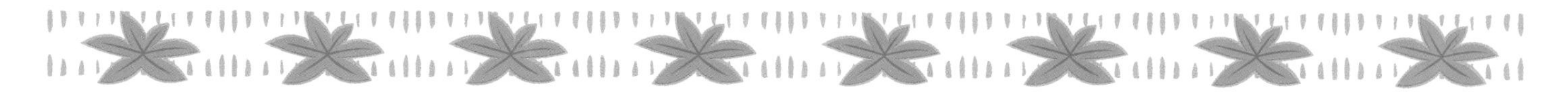

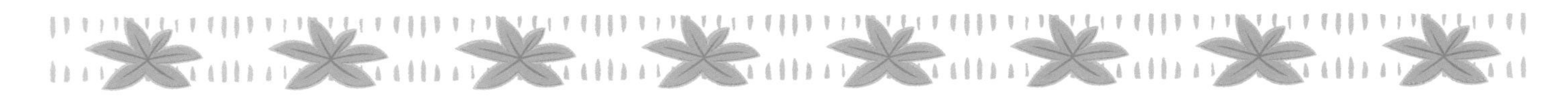

Hiss! Hiss! Aladar and Plio looked upward. Something strange was happening. Birds squawked overhead and the lemurs chittered wildly as a meteor shower began. They had never seen anything like it!

"Something is wrong," warned Yar, sniffing the air. The rumbling sounds were growing louder and louder.

"Where's Suri?" asked Plio, desperately looking around for her child.

At that moment, they saw a huge fireball hit the earth. The force of the impact was so great that it caused a tidal wave, which was rolling toward them faster and faster.

"Run, Aladar, run!" Plio cried from Aladar's back as the dinosaur ran toward the trees to find her little Suri.

Aladar ran as fast as he could, carrying his lemur family to safety. When they reached the cliff, they took a deep breath and jumped into the water below. Aladar and the lemurs swam to the surface and clung to each other until they were safely on dry land. Exhausted, they looked back. Their island had been destroyed.

"Come on," Aladar said. "We can't stay here." So they began to move, uncertain about their destination, but knowing that they must find a new place to live. They didn't know what had happened, but they knew that things would never be the same.

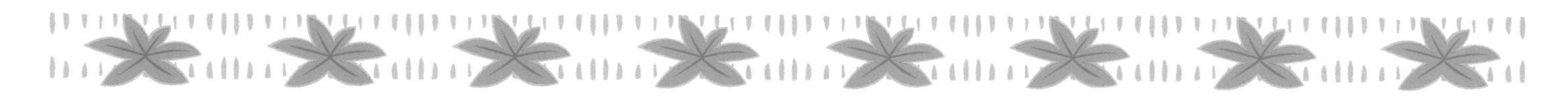

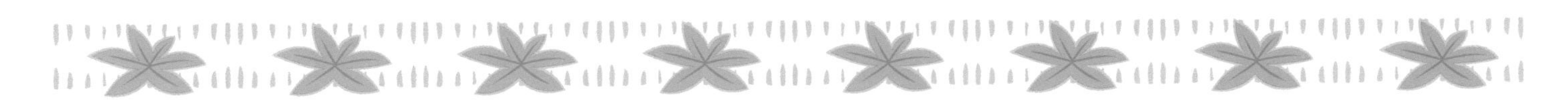

They walked for miles and miles. Eventually, they came across a herd of various dinosaurs who were on a journey of their own. The herd was headed to the Nesting Grounds.

The leader of the herd was an iguanodon named Kron. He was a tough dinosaur who pushed the herd on relentlessly. Kron had a sister. Her name was Neera, and Aladar thought she was beautiful.

"Keep those legs moving or you'll get left behind," cautioned a feisty styracosaur named Eema. Also in the group was an elderly brachiosaur named Baylene who had a difficult time keeping up with the herd.

They struggled to keep going as they crossed the desert. Suddenly, Eema cried, "The lake is over the hill! We made it!" But looking over the hill, they were shocked to see that the lake was dry.

Fortunately, Aladar made a discovery. When Baylene pressed her humongous foot into the sand, water sprang up from underground. Aladar made sure that the younger dinosaurs got plenty of water to drink.

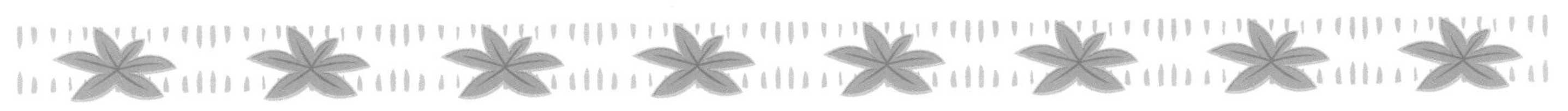

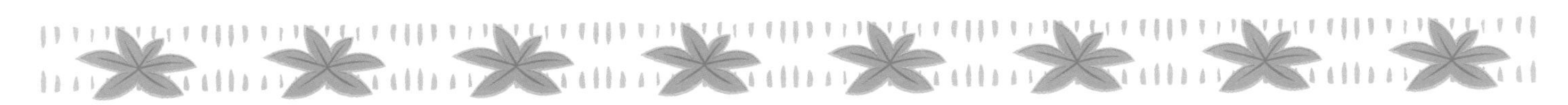

As they continued on their journey, the dinosaurs kept a careful watch for the dangerous carnotaurs lurking in the area.

"Move!" ordered Kron.

"What's wrong? Why are we moving?" asked Aladar.

"It's the carnotaurs. They've got a mouthful of teeth and a very bad attitude," replied Eema as they fell further behind the rest of the herd.

Aladar sighed. They would never catch up. The stragglers soon came across Bruton, Kron's chief lieutenant, who had been injured and left behind. Aladar invited Bruton to join them in the cave where they decided to seek shelter.

"Come on. On your feet," he said, helping Bruton to the cave.

Bruton couldn't understand why Aladar continued to encourage the others. "Why is he pushing them on with false hope?" he asked Plio.

"It's hope that has gotten us this far," she replied.

Outside, the carnotaurs picked up the scent. When they attacked, Bruton bravely held them off so that Aladar and the others could escape.

Running through the cave, Aladar refused to give up — until they met a dead end. "I guess we're not meant to survive," he sighed.

"Shame on you," said Baylene as she kicked the wall of rocks. "I'm not dying here." When the others joined in, they broke through! They strode out of the cave and into the glorious sunlight of the Nesting Grounds.

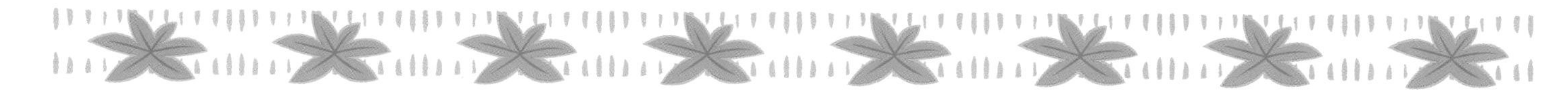

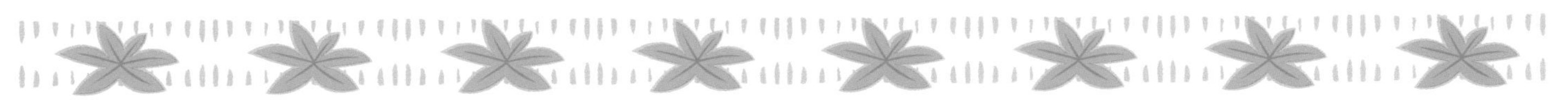

Looking around, Aladar saw that the usual path to the Nesting Grounds was blocked. The only way in was through the cave they had just come from. Aladar retraced his steps and soon found the herd again.

"The carnotaurs are coming!" he cried. "Follow me! There's a safer way to the Nesting Grounds."

Kron, furious that his leadership might be questioned, attacked Aladar. Fortunately, Neera came to Aladar's rescue. Neera's faith in Aladar was enough for the rest of the herd, and they turned to follow him. Suddenly, however, they were face to face with a carnotaur. Aladar stood his ground and the rest of the herd rallied behind him.Their attacker backed down.

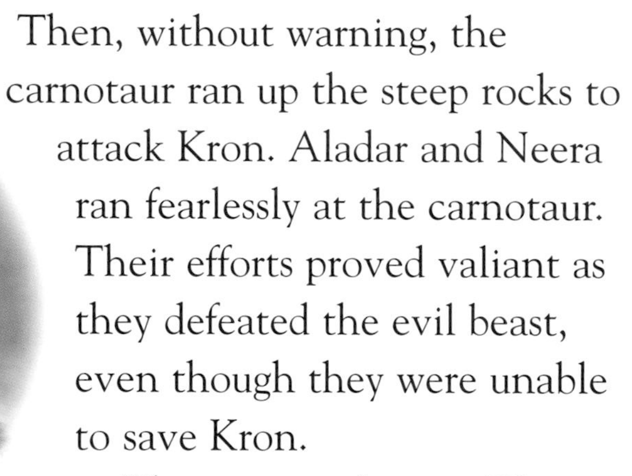

Then, without warning, the carnotaur ran up the steep rocks to attack Kron. Aladar and Neera ran fearlessly at the carnotaur. Their efforts proved valiant as they defeated the evil beast, even though they were unable to save Kron.

They were safe now. The herd gladly followed Aladar to the Nesting Grounds.

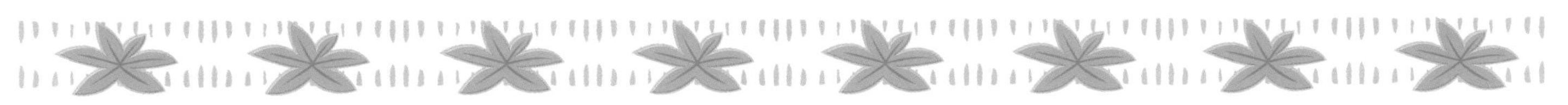

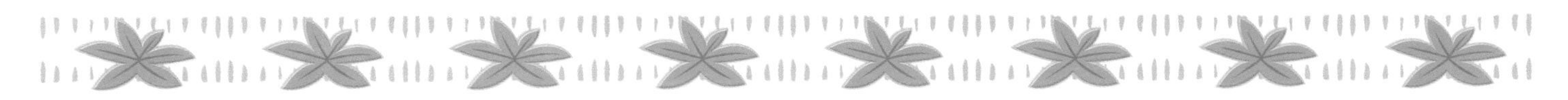

Time passed quickly in their new surroundings. It was a beautiful place to play and live, with green grass and blue water. It wasn't long before Aladar gathered with his family and friends as they watched over the eggs that were about to hatch.

One dinosaur egg began to crack open ever so slowly.

"Look! Somebody wants to meet you," said Plio. The motherly lemur thought it was the sweetest little thing she had ever laid eyes on.

"Let me get a good look," said Yar. Picking up the little one, Yar remembered the day he and Plio had first met Aladar. They had been through so much together, and life was good for them now.

Aladar raised up and bellowed as loudly as he could, celebrating the new life and the love of his family and friends.

Who would have predicted that such a small dinosaur egg could change the lives of so many and give them so much happiness!

Peter Pan

Adapted by Kate Hannigan

In a cozy house on a quiet street in the busy city of London, there lived three children named Wendy, John, and Michael Darling. The children loved to tell stories about the brave Peter Pan and a magical place called Never Land.

Some people believed that Peter Pan was the spirit of youth. But Wendy, John, and Michael believed that Peter was a real person. The boys made Peter Pan the hero of their games.

"Take that, Captain Hook! And that!" the boys would shout.

The room was quiet when the window opened and someone flew inside. It was Peter Pan!

Peter and Tinker Bell were searching for Peter's lost shadow. They noisily chased it around the room, waking up Wendy.

Wendy was thrilled to discover the visitors. She grabbed a needle and thread and stitched the shadow to the tips of Peter's toes so that he would never lose it again.

Peter asked Wendy to come with him to Never Land, where no one ever had to grow up. She was thrilled!

John and Michael thought it sounded wonderful, too. But how would they get there?

Peter said that they would fly, of course. And with a sprinkling of pixie dust from Tinker Bell, Peter and the children flew out the window and over the yard.

"We're off to Never Land!" shouted Peter Pan.

Wendy, John, and Michael flapped their arms. They soared high above the rooftops and past London's famous clock tower. The city looked so tiny to the children from so high up in the sky. They flew on and on into the night sky until they reached Never Land.

Peter, Tinker Bell, and the children perched on a high cloud and gazed down at Never Land. Peter was excited to show them Mermaid Lagoon and Blindman's Bluff. But there, in the waters of Pirate's Cove, was the dreaded Captain Hook!

Years ago, a crocodile had gotten a taste of Captain Hook's hand during a swordfight with Peter Pan. Hook blamed Peter for it and had been trying to capture him ever since. The two things Hook disliked most in this world were that crocodile and Peter Pan.

The children were eager to explore Never Land with Peter and Tinker Bell. But Tinker Bell was not being nice to Wendy, so Peter banished Tink from the island for one week.

Peter took Wendy to Mermaid Lagoon. Michael and John played follow the leader with the Lost Boys. The Lost Boys were children who had come to live with Peter in Never Land.

As Wendy met the mermaids, Captain Hook paddled by in a small boat. He had captured Tiger Lily, the Indian princess! Peter and Wendy followed them. But they weren't the only ones. Swimming behind Hook's boat was the hungry crocodile.

Captain Hook demanded that Tiger Lily reveal Peter Pan's hideaway. Tiger Lily wouldn't tell Hook anything. Peter decided to rescue the princess, so he began to play tricks on Hook.

Peter flew into the air, swooping and spinning. He and Captain Hook battled up and down Skull Rock. Peter prevailed, and Hook splashed into the water below. The crocodile chased Captain Hook all the way back to his ship.

Meanwhile, the Indian Chief was worried about Tiger Lily. When Peter Pan rescued Tiger Lily, the Indian Chief was so happy that he threw a great, big party for Peter and the children.

Meanwhile, Captain Hook found Tinker Bell and tricked her into showing him the way to the hideaway. After she did, Hook threw Tinker Bell into a glass case and locked the door.

Captain Hook and the pirates raced to the hideaway. They hid in the bushes nearby and waited for the right moment.

Inside, the children and the Lost Boys were getting homesick. But Peter wanted them to stay in Never Land.

The children left the hideaway without Peter only to find Captain Hook and the pirates waiting for them. The children were captured and taken back to Hook's ship.

"Peter Pan will save us," Wendy said as she bravely walked the plank. Sure enough, Peter Pan appeared and caught Wendy just before she splashed into the water.

"Now you've gone too far, Hook!" Peter shouted from high atop the ship. Hook responded by drawing his sword.

Peter Pan swooped down and freed John, Michael, and the Lost Boys. The children bravely battled the pirates while Peter went after Hook. The wicked captain waved his hook and chased Peter Pan up and down the ship.

"Come back here, you coward!" shouted Hook. Peter said that nobody called him a coward and got away with it. He fought Hook with all his might, jumping and jabbing, leaping and lunging.

Finally, it was clear that Peter had beaten Hook. Peter was too quick for Hook. He had Hook cornered. Peter, being the good sport that he was, told Hook that he was free to go. But Captain Hook was a cheater, and he made one last jab at Peter Pan.

Hook's feet slipped, and he plunged into the ocean below. The Captain soon realized that he wasn't alone in the water. The hungry crocodile was waiting for him. It opened its big jaws and swallowed Captain Hook in a single gulp!

Captain Hook let out a yell and pushed open the crocodile's jaws from inside its mouth. He ran right back out of its mouth and paddled as fast as he could to get away. Captain Hook raced through the water with the hungry crocodile snapping its jaws behind him.

The children laughed and cheered as they watched Captain Hook swim into the distance. Peter Pan had come through and saved the day.

It was time for Wendy, John, and Michael to return home. With a sprinkling of pixie dust from Tinker Bell, Peter Pan gently sailed the ship carrying the children back to London.

No sooner had the children drifted off to sleep when their parents quietly opened the nursery door to check on the them. John and Michael were tucked in their beds, but Wendy was asleep at the window.

Wendy yawned and told her mother and father they had just gotten back. As Wendy began to explain, she gazed dreamily out the window at the full moon and Peter Pan's pirate ship slowly sailing across it.

Wendy's parents stared out the window. They couldn't believe their eyes! Father said he had the strangest feeling he'd seen that ship before. It was long ago, he told Wendy, when he was very young.

MULAN

Story adapted by Lynne Roberts

Life in China was about to change. The Huns had crossed over the Great Wall of China and wanted to battle the Chinese for their land. The Huns were a group of traveling warriors. They would move from country to country and battle any army they encountered. As it turns out, they did not like the Chinese or their Great Wall. The Huns were ready to attack each village, one by one.

General Li, of the Chinese Emperor's Army, rode as fast as he could to tell the Emperor that the Huns had crossed the wall. General Li knew that China was in danger. Only the Emperor would know how to save the people of China.

When the Emperor heard the news, he was very concerned. It had been a long time since he had sent his men into battle. He told General Li that new armies must be assembled. Every family in China must help fight the war against the Huns.

"One grain of rice can tip the scale," said the Emperor. He knew that each man who fought in the war would make a difference in the end.

Meanwhile, the evil Shan-Yu had begun to frighten the people of China. He used violence against anyone who got in his way, and he set whole villages on fire. Shan-Yu was the most powerful leader of the Huns. He did not like the Emperor of China.

In a small village, a young girl named Fa Mulan was preparing to meet the town's Matchmaker. The Matchmaker met with the young ladies of the village to decide who was ready to be married. Everyone in Mulan's family hoped that the Matchmaker would find a husband for Mulan. But Mulan needed to be refined, poised, and punctual when she met the Matchmaker. Unfortunately, Mulan was late.

Mulan's mother and grandmother helped her get dressed. They put on her makeup and fixed her hair. Grandmother gave Mulan an apple for serenity, jade beads for beauty, a pendant for balance, and a cricket for luck. The cricket's name was Cri-Kee. Mulan then jumped on her horse and quickly rode to the Matchmaker's house.

Mulan was nervous about meeting the Matchmaker. She wanted to bring honor to her family. She did not want to let her father down and shame the family name. But when she met the Matchmaker, everything went wrong! Mulan had written notes on her arm so that she would not forget the right things to say, but the Matchmaker touched the ink and got it on her face. Then Cri-Kee made Mulan spill the tea, and the Matchmaker slipped and sat on hot coals. Mulan was blamed for everything!

"She will never bring your family honor!" yelled the Matchmaker. Mulan and her family were very upset.

Back at home, Mulan talked with her father. Mulan was afraid that she would never be the perfect bride or the perfect daughter. Her father smiled and told her that she was just a late bloomer. He had hope for his daughter.

Just then, a traveling messenger from the Emperor arrived with an announcement. He told of the war with the Huns and declared that one man from each family was required to help fight. Fa Zhou, Mulan's father, was the only man in the family. He would have to go. Mulan was upset. Fa Zhou had been a hero in the last Chinese war, where he injured his leg.

That night, Mulan snuck out of bed. She took her father's armor and sword and cut her hair so that she would look like a boy. She leaped on her horse, Khan, and rode off to fight in her father's place. She could not bear to think of her injured father in the war.

When Mulan got to the training camp, she had trouble making friends. She tried to act like a man, but her awkward behavior caused problems. She was so clumsy that even Captain Li Shang, could not believe his eyes!

After weeks of practice, Mulan learned to be a good soldier. She had some help from Cri-Kee and Mushu. Mushu was the tiny dragon sent by Mulan's ancestors to help and protect Mulan. He vowed to help make Mulan into an honorable soldier.

The time came for Mulan's troop to head into battle. As they rode toward the front line, they were saddened to see the villages that the Huns had burned. So many people were gone because of Shan-Yu and the evil Hun army.

Over a snowy mountaintop, Mulan and the other soldiers came face to face with the Huns. There were hundreds of them! Shan-Yu and his troops came thundering down the mountain. Li Shang and his troops were vastly outnumbered. But Mulan had an idea. She pointed and fired a cannon at a snowy peak that hung over the mountain. The blast caused an avalanche, leaving the Huns buried in the snow!

Mulan saved her troops from the Huns, but now she, Li Shang, and Khan were in danger. The avalanche had forced them to the edge of the mountain. They were saved by Mulan's quick thinking and the strength of her friends.

Li Shang and the troops were very proud of Mulan. But they were worried when they saw that she was hurt! Shan-Yu had grazed Mulan with his sword as she lit the cannon.

The troop's doctor treated her wound, but he also discovered her secret. He had no choice but to tell Li Shang and the others that Mulan was really a girl! Shang was angry to learn that he had been tricked. The penalty for such a lie was severe in China, but Li Shang spared Mulan's life. Mulan had saved Shang in battle, now it was Shang's turn to save Mulan. Shang left her and Khan on the mountain, alone but alive.

At the Emperor's palace, there was a big celebration. Shang and his troops were being honored for defeating the Huns. Everyone was happy that China was safe again. But Shang and his troops rode with heavy hearts as they knew that Mulan was the true hero.

On the snowy mountain, though, the Huns were still alive! Mulan saw Shan-Yu and his men crawl out from under the snow. She knew that she had to warn Shang and the Emperor. She rode quickly to the palace.

Nobody believed Mulan's story. She was back to being just a girl. She tried to warn Li Shang, but he was still angry with her.

The Huns arrived at the palace in the middle of the celebration. They had snuck down from the mountain and hid upon the top of the palace. Everyone was terrified as the Huns grabbed the Emperor and took him up to the balcony of the palace. Mulan knew she had to save him. She told Li Shang and the troops that she had a plan.

Mulan told several of the men in the troop to dress like women. They all snuck into the palace. The Huns that were guarding the door were fooled. They liked the attention they were getting from these women, and they let their weapons down. Mulan and her friends attacked! They broke through the palace door and saved the Emperor from the grips of Shan-Yu.

After the men hustled the Emperor to saftey, Mulan found herself trapped on the roof of the palace with Shan-Yu. Mushu the dragon was in a nearby tower. The tower held fireworks that were to be used for the victory celebration. He strapped himself to a big rocket and aimed it at Shan-Yu. The Huns were defeated.

With her quick thinking and the help of her friends, Mulan had saved China and the Emperor. The Emperor was extremely grateful. He gave Mulan a crest of honor to show what she had done for him and the sword of Shan-Yu to show what she had done for China. Never before had a woman been so honored in China.

Mulan was thrilled to receive the recognition that the Emperor gave her, but she really wanted to be with her family again. When she returned home, her father was very proud of her.

"The greatest gift and honor is having you for a daughter," Fa Zhou told Mulan as he gave her a hug.

Li Shang was still at the palace. The Emperor could tell that Li Shang was in love with Mulan. He told Li Shang that Mulan was a very special girl and that he should find her and be with her.

Li Shang went to Mulan's home. Mulan's mother and grandmother were very impressed by the great warrior. They giggled with excitement as they watched him approach Mulan. Mulan was surprised but very happy to see him. She asked him to stay for dinner, for she had fallen in love with him, too.

There isn't a matchmaker in the world who could have done better.

Story adapted by Kate Hannigan

It was a sunny afternoon, and Alice sat with her kitten, Dinah, on the branches of a big tree. Her sister was reading a story.

Alice wasn't really listening. She began to drift off, imagining what things would be like if she had a world of her own.

Suddenly a white rabbit scurried past. But this was no ordinary rabbit. This rabbit was wearing a jacket and bow tie. He was also carrying a large gold pocket watch in one hand and an umbrella in the other.

"I'm late!" said the White Rabbit. He quickly dashed down the path and into the woods.

Alice thought the rabbit might be late for something fun, like a party. So she chased after him.

She hopscotched across a stream and called out to him.

"Wait for me, Mr. Rabbit," she said. "Could you please slow down?"

The White Rabbit quickly scampered into a rabbit hole, and Alice went in right behind him.

12
1
2
3
4
5
6
7
8
9
10
11

Alice tumbled down the rabbit hole, landing gently at the bottom. She followed the rabbit through a small door that led to an even smaller door.

Alice tugged on the doorknob and heard a voice. The doorknob was speaking to Alice! He said that Alice was too big to pass through the little door and that she should drink from the bottle on the table.

The label said "Drink me," so Alice did. With each sip, Alice got smaller and smaller until she was just the right size to get through the door.

"Perfect," said Alice, only to discover that the door was locked. The key was on the table high above her. Alice wondered how she would ever reach the key. The doorknob suggested she try eating a cookie from the box nearby. A note on the cookie said, "Eat me," so Alice did.

Alice grew bigger and bigger until she bumped her head on the ceiling! Alice cried huge tears that flooded the room. The doorknob told Alice to take another drink.

In one gulp, Alice was small again. She slipped into the empty bottle and floated through the keyhole.

On the other side of the door, Alice saw a world of strange things. There were birds that could talk and fish that could dance. And she met silly twins called Tweedledee and Tweedledum.

The twins bounced and spun and firmly shook Alice's hands. They sat her down on a log and taught her a lesson about manners. Alice had a lovely time, but she was eager to find the White Rabbit. So she said good-bye and went on her way.

Soon she found the White Rabbit in his house near the woods. He was searching for his white gloves and asked Alice to help him. As she looked around his room, she came across more cookies with notes that said, "Eat me." So Alice did.

With one bite, Alice grew. She grew and she grew and she grew. Her legs popped out of the doors and stretched into the yard. Her arms burst through the upstairs windows. Her head reached the rooftop.

Alice was enormous! The White Rabbit thought she was a monster and wanted to chase her out. Alice looked for a way to escape. She spotted a garden in the yard and thought perhaps eating one of its vegetables would help. She reached down with her giant hand and pulled up a bright orange carrot. She ate the carrot in one bite. Thankfully, it worked and Alice shrank. She shrank so much that she was smaller than her normal size.

The White Rabbit dashed off. Alice tried to chase him, but she was too tiny. Luckily, she met a caterpillar who told her to take a bite of a mushroom. That made Alice grow bigger until she was the perfect size. She saved some in her pockets for later.

As Alice walked on in search of the White Rabbit, she saw a sliver of moon in the sky. But it wasn't really the moon—it was the Cheshire Cat's smile! He pointed Alice toward a clearing amongst the trees.

Alice followed the sounds of singing and came across a most unusual tea party. The table was covered with dancing teapots. At the end of the table sat two curious creatures drinking tea. They were the Mad Hatter and the March Hare!

Alice joined their birthday party. But it wasn't actually a birthday party, they told her. It was an unbirthday party.

"We only get one birthday a year," they said. "But there are 364 unbirthdays!"

Alice told them it was her unbirthday, too. So they gave her a cake with a candle that sparkled.

Alice was getting tired of looking for the White Rabbit. She wanted to go home. She looked up and saw the crescent moon shining above her. It was the Cheshire Cat again! He told Alice she shouldn't go home until she met the Queen of Hearts.

Alice grew excited—she'd never met a queen before. The Cheshire Cat showed her the way. Alice skipped down the path to meet the Queen.

Suddenly trumpets blared, and the White Rabbit appeared. He announced the arrival of the Queen of Hearts and her tiny husband, the King. "Her royal majesty, the Queen of Hearts!" the White Rabbit choked.

Alice thought the Queen was bossy. She wanted everything her way. When she didn't get it, she shrieked, "Off with his head!"

The Cheshire Cat appeared and played a trick on the Queen. The Queen was furious and thought Alice was responsible for the trick.

The Queen screeched, "Off with her … !" The King interrupted and suggested they have a trial, so everyone went to the Queen's court.

The White Rabbit read the charges. The March Hare and the Mad Hatter were there, too. Alice thought the whole thing was ridiculous!

Alice reached into her pocket and found a bit of the mushroom she had saved. She took a bite and grew so big that she banged her head on the ceiling of the Queen's court.

Since she was so big, Alice wasn't afraid to scold the Queen. "You're not a queen!" Alice shouted. "You're just a bad-tempered old tyrant!"

Alice didn't know it, but as she shouted at the Queen, she was shrinking smaller and smaller. When she finished yelling, the Queen was red with anger. Alice was back to her old size.

"Off with her head!" screamed the Queen.

Alice ran away as fast as she could. The Mad Hatter and the March Hare ran after her. And all the creatures at court began to chase her, too.

"I must get home quickly," she said to herself. "I must hurry! Hurry!"

Finally, she heard a voice say, "Alice, what are you talking about?"

Alice opened her eyes and saw her sister standing over her. On her lap was a sleeping kitten. Alice was happy to see it wasn't the Cheshire Cat. It was Dinah! Alice hugged her tight and smiled.

It had all been an incredible dream.

Lady and the TRAMP

Story adapted by Kate Hannigan

On a snowy night in a sleepy little town, a colorful present sat under a Christmas tree.

"It's for you, Darling," said Jim Dear.

As Darling untied the pretty ribbon, a nose and two eyes peeked out. It was a puppy! Darling clapped her hands. "What a beautiful little lady," she said. And that's what they named her: Lady.

Lady loved living with Jim Dear and Darling. She slept on their bed at night and brought them the newspaper in the morning. Life was good.

One day, things started to change. Darling didn't want to go on walks anymore. And Jim Dear no longer wanted to race with Lady.

Lady asked her friends, Jock and Trusty, if they knew what was happening. Both dogs nodded. They told her that her humans were having a baby.

Just then a scruffy, cocky street dog named Tramp walked into the yard.

"When the baby moves in," warned Tramp, "the dog moves out."

Before long, the baby arrived. Jim Dear ran through the house shouting, "It's a boy! It's a boy!" Lady knew immediately how important the new baby was to Jim Dear and Darling.

Lady had never seen a baby, so she quietly crept into the nursery where Darling was singing and humming. Jim Dear picked up Lady and let her peek into the crib. There it was, a tiny, newborn baby. Lady had never seen anything so adorable.

Lady fell in love with it. Now she had another human to take care of.

Not long after the baby's arrival, Jim Dear and Darling had to take a trip. They told Lady she could help Aunt Sarah care for the baby. Lady was determined to do a good job of babysitting.

But when Aunt Sarah arrived, she wanted nothing to do with Lady. Aunt Sarah didn't like the idea of a dog around the baby. In fact, Aunt Sarah didn't like dogs at all. She liked cats!

Lady heard a muffled sound coming from Aunt Sarah's suitcase. She poked her nose around the bag and, suddenly, two tails flicked out. Cats! Aunt Sarah had brought her two Siamese cats with her.

The cats got into everything. They scared the bird and knocked over the fishbowl. Lady tried to keep them from making a mess of things, but it was no use. The more she barked at the cats, the angrier Aunt Sarah became. Lady just couldn't win.

Aunt Sarah took Lady down to the pet store. She asked the owner for a good, strong muzzle to put over Lady's mouth. Aunt Sarah paid the shopkeeper and strapped the muzzle onto Lady's head.

Lady was afraid of the muzzle. She ran from the pet store. She raced down the street as fast as she could while still wearing it. She tried and tried, but she couldn't get the muzzle off.

A pack of mean dogs chased after Lady. She was so frightened, she ran down an alley and hid behind a barrel. At the last moment, Tramp came out of nowhere. He jumped in front of the dogs and chased them away. He saved Lady's life!

Tramp saw the muzzle and felt sorry for Lady. "We've got to get this thing off you," he told her.

Tramp took Lady to the zoo. He thought that maybe one of the animals there could help.

They looked at the apes. "They're too much like humans," said Tramp.

They looked at the alligators. "They're too hungry!" said Tramp.

Finally they came across a beaver who was busily chewing through a piece of wood. "He's perfect," Tramp said.

In no time, the beaver bit right through the strap on Lady's muzzle. Lady was free!

Lady was very happy to have the muzzle off. She and Tramp wanted to celebrate. They walked through the town and stopped at Tramp's favorite place, Tony's Italian Restaurant.

Tramp barked at the back door and Tony came out. Tramp introduced Tony to his new friend, Lady. Tony smiled and whispered to Tramp.

"You should settle down with this one," Tony said. "She's beautiful!"

Tony hollered into the kitchen to make a special dinner for Tramp and Lady. Spaghetti and meatballs!

Lady and Tramp slurped the spaghetti as Tony and Joe played romantic music and sang romantic songs for the couple.

The two dogs gazed into each other's eyes. Tramp even gave Lady the last meatball. It was love.

Lady and Tramp walked through the park in the moonlight. Finally, Lady said she had to go home.

"Let's have some fun first," said Tramp. And he slipped under a fence and began to chase some chickens around their coop.

Lady ran after him, and together they raised quite a ruckus!

Lady and Tramp slipped through the fence to get away from the squawking chickens just as the dogcatcher appeared.

Tramp ran as fast as he could, racing down alleys and through a field. Finally he stopped for a rest. “Phew!” he said. “That was a close one, Lady!”

He turned around, but Lady wasn’t there. Tramp ran back toward the chicken yard, but he couldn’t find her. The dogcatcher had caught Lady! She was furious at Tramp for getting her into this predicament.

Lady spent the rest of the day at the pound. Finally, she was allowed to go home. But Aunt Sarah made her sleep outside, chained to the doghouse.

Lady was miserable. Jock and Trusty stopped by to cheer her up. Tramp crept through the fence and gave Lady a bone as a gift. But Lady was angry with Tramp for getting her into trouble.

“Good-bye,” she huffed, turning her back on Tramp. “And take that bone with you!”

Tramp left, and Lady was all alone in the quiet yard. It grew dark, and the rain began to fall.

Lady lay down in her doghouse and looked up at the big house. She wished she were inside with her family.

Suddenly, Lady saw something move in the darkness. It was a rat!

Lady barked and jumped after the rat, but she couldn't reach it. She was chained to the doghouse. But Tramp heard Lady's barking and ran back to help. Lady told him the rat had run into the house!

"You've got to save the baby," Lady said.

Tramp scrambled into the house chasing after the rat. He cornered it in the baby's room, and they fought wildly. Lady finally broke free from the chain and raced after them. Lady and Tramp bravely battled the rat, waking the baby, and Aunt Sarah, too.

"You mongrels," shouted Aunt Sarah. She locked Lady in the basement and called the dogcatcher to take away Tramp.

Jim Dear and Darling came home just as Tramp was being put into the dogcatcher's wagon. They ran inside to find out what was happening.

"Lady, I think you and your friend were trying to save the baby," said Jim Dear when he found the dead rat.

Lady and Jim Dear raced after the dogcatcher.

CITY
POUND

Jock and Trusty ran after the dogcatcher as well. There was no time to waste! Trusty barked at the horses to stop the wagon, but it startled them. They jumped in fright, turning the wagon over. Lady and Jim Dear were able to rescue Tramp from the dogcatcher just in time.

Tramp loved Lady. And Lady loved Tramp. They decided to settle down together with her humans in the cozy old house.

Jim Dear and Darling grew to love Tramp as much as they loved Lady. Before long, Lady and Tramp's family began to grow. They had four healthy puppies who looked just like them. Lady and Tramp adored Jim Dear, Darling, and the baby. And they were happy with their precious puppies.

With Tramp, Lady had learned what it was like to be a carefree dog roaming around town. And with Lady, Tramp had finally learned what it meant to have a family of his own.

THE LION KING

Story adapted by Susan Rich Brooke

The sun rose over the African plain, just as it had done every morning since the beginning of time. But this morning was special. Across the vast Pride Lands, herds of animals journeyed to Pride Rock to celebrate the birth of King Mufasa's and Queen Sarabi's son.

Rafiki, the wise old baboon, carried the lion cub to the edge of the rock and held him up high. Zebras, antelopes, giraffes, and elephants all knelt before their new prince, Simba.

But one animal—Mufasa's brother, Scar—was too angry to celebrate. If Simba had not been born, Scar would have been next in line to be king. He was determined to be king somehow.

When Simba grew a little older, Mufasa led him back to the top of Pride Rock. "Simba, look," said Mufasa, as the sun edged over the horizon. "Everything the light touches is part of our kingdom. A king's time as a ruler rises and falls like the sun. One day, the sun will set on my time here and rise with you as the new king."

"And this will all be mine? Wow!" said Simba, looking around. "But what about that shadowy place?"

"That is beyond our borders," warned Mufasa. "You must never go there, Simba."

Simba was in awe of the land. He knew he'd make a great king one day.

Just then Zazu, the King's helper, arrived with the morning report. "Sire!" he said to Mufasa. "Hyenas have crossed into the Pride Lands!" This was business that needed his attention, so Mufasa sent Simba home and swiftly ran after the dark shapes in the distance.

Simba saw Scar sunning himself on a rock. "Hey, Uncle Scar!" Simba cried. He was still excited after his talk with Mufasa. "My dad just showed me the whole kingdom, and I'm going to rule it all!"

Simba's words gave Scar an idea. Maybe he could trick the cub into going to the dangerous place. "Did your father show you what's beyond the border?" Scar asked Simba.

"No," said Simba. "He said I can't go there."

"He's absolutely right," Scar replied, grinning slyly. "Only the bravest of lions go there. An elephant graveyard is no place for a young prince."

"An elephant what?" said Simba. "Wow!"

Simba remembered his father's warning. But wouldn't Dad be proud of such a brave cub? Of course he would, thought Simba. So he decided to go, and he asked his friend Nala to join him.

When Simba's mother saw the two cubs going off to play, she sent Zazu along to keep an eye on them. But Simba and Nala scampered across the plains so fast that soon Zazu was trailing behind.

Happy to be free of Zazu, Simba leapt toward Nala. Playfully, she flipped Simba onto his back. They continued to wrestle until the two cubs tumbled down a hill and landed with a thud. They were startled to find a huge elephant skull right next to them.

"Let's check it out!" said Simba. But before they had a chance, Zazu caught up and scolded them.

Suddenly, three hyenas popped out of the skull! Flashing their sharp teeth, the hyenas raced after the cubs and trapped them inside the bones of an elephant's rib cage.

Then out of nowhere, a giant paw smacked the hyenas and sent them flying onto a pile of bones. The paw belonged to Mufasa. "If you ever come near my son again . . . ," warned the mighty lion without finishing his threat.

Mufasa sent Nala and Zazu home so he could talk to Simba alone.

"Being brave doesn't mean you go looking for trouble," Mufasa told his mischievous cub.

Overhead, bright stars began to dot the evening sky. "We'll always be together, right?" Simba asked his father.

"Simba, let me tell you what my father told me," Mufasa replied. He gestured toward the sky as he began to speak. "Look at the stars. The great kings of the past look down on us from those stars. They will always be there to guide you, and so will I."

Scar's plan to get rid of Simba had failed. But he had another idea. The next day, Scar said to Simba, "Your father has a surprise for you." Scar led the cub down a steep gorge, where a herd of wildebeests was stampeding. Simba clung fearfully to a branch to escape the dangerous hooves. Suddenly, Mufasa appeared and snatched his son away to safety.

As Mufasa tried to climb up the gorge, the rocky wall started to crumble. Mufasa reached out to his brother. But instead of helping him, Scar let the mighty King fall. Mufasa was gone.

"Run away, Simba, and never return!" yelled Scar. Simba ran, and Scar sent the hyenas to chase him. With Mufasa gone and the belief that Simba would be gone, too, Scar went to Pride Rock to take over the kingdom.

But Simba was alive. The hyenas had been too scared to follow him through some thorns. Exhausted, Simba fell asleep. When he awoke, he saw a friendly meerkat named Timon and a fun-loving warthog named Pumbaa. With nowhere else to go, Simba went home with them.

In the company of his new friends, Simba grew up to be a young lion. One night, while they gazed at the stars, Simba said, "Someone once told me that the great kings of the past are up there watching over us."

Pumbaa and Timon laughed. "Who told you a crazy thing like that?" Timon asked. Simba, thinking of his father, was silent.

The next day, Simba heard a call for help. Pumbaa was caught beneath the trunk of a fallen tree, and Timon was trying to protect him from a hungry young lioness. To Simba's surprise, the lioness was Nala!

"Everyone thinks you're dead," Nala said. "But you're alive! That means you're the king!" Nala told Simba that Scar had let the hyenas take over the Pride Lands. Everything was destroyed. There was no food and no water.

"Simba, if you don't do something soon, everyone will starve," Nala pleaded. But Simba refused. He liked having no responsibilities.

"You're not the Simba I remember," Nala said sadly as Simba walked away.

That night, while the others slept, Simba gazed up at the twinkling sky. "I won't go back," he said. "It won't change anything." Suddenly, the wise baboon Rafiki appeared.

"Who are you?" Simba asked.

"The question is: Who are you?" said Rafiki. When Simba didn't answer, Rafiki added, "I know your father." The old baboon led Simba to a clear, smooth pool and told him to look down. Simba stared at the pool and his father's face appeared. "You see?" said Rafiki. "He lives in you." Simba lifted his eyes and saw the image of his father in the stars.

"Remember who you are, Simba," said his father's image. "You are my son and the one true king!" Then his father was gone. Simba sat alone on a rock, thinking.

When Nala, Timon, and Pumbaa woke up the next morning, they looked all over for Simba. "You won't find him here," Rafiki told them. "The king has returned!"

The three friends hurried toward the Pride Lands. Ahead of them, Simba had already reached Pride Rock. The once beautiful homeland was now in ruins. Something needed to be done quickly. Simba looked for his mother and found her quarreling with Scar.

"This is my kingdom!" Simba roared. "Step down, Scar."

Scar was shocked that his nephew was still alive. He didn't waste any time trying to keep Simba away. He quickly sent the hyenas after Simba. They chased Simba off Pride Rock and left him clinging to the edge. Gathering all his strength, Simba leaped toward his uncle. Simba chased Scar off Pride Rock. This time, Scar clung to the edge.

"Run away! Run away and never return!" Simba commanded Scar. But instead Scar lunged at Simba. Simba had no choice but to hurl him off the cliff. This time, it was Scar who was gone.

Under King Simba's rule, the Pride Lands flourished. The herds returned to graze, and food was plentiful once more. Everyone felt lucky to have Simba as their king.

Soon the animals gathered again to celebrate the birth of the king's daughter. Simba and Nala watched proudly as Rafiki held their cub high over Pride Rock. There were good times ahead for everyone in the land.

The Aristocats

Story adapted by Lora Kalkman

Once upon a time, in a grand mansion in Paris, there lived a beautiful white Persian cat. Her name was Duchess. Duchess was the proud mother of three delightful kittens. Toulouse had orange fur, Berlioz was gray, and Marie had fur as white as her mother's. Their owner, Madame Adelaide, generously cared for them. She made sure they were well-versed in art and music. The kittens also loved to run and play.

Because Madame loved her cats so dearly, she was careful to plan for their future. She had her lawyer prepare a will. She planned to leave her vast fortune to her cats. Once the cats' lifetime was over, the fortune would go to Edgar, her loyal butler. He had worked for Madame for many years.

Edgar happened to overhear Madame's plans for her will. He was absolutely astonished. When Edgar considered that cats have nine lives, he became particularly upset. If the cats lived about 15 years for each of their nine lives, it would be 135 years before he'd see any money. He decided the only way he would ever get the inheritance was to make the cats disappear.

That night, Duchess and the kittens enjoyed their usual bowl of cream. What they didn't realize was that Edgar had added a sleeping potion to their meal. Soon, they all fell fast asleep. So did their friend, an adorable little mouse named Roquefort, who'd dipped his cracker in the tainted cream. Duchess and the kittens slept soundly, unaware that they were about to be taken on an adventure against their will.

Edgar put the sleeping cats into a basket. Toulouse briefly opened his eyes, catching a glimpse of the greedy butler, but soon drifted back to sleep. With the cats in tow, Edgar set off for the country on his motorbike. If the cats were lost in the country, he reasoned, he would not have to wait to collect Madame's fortune.

Without warning, Edgar was startled by two hound dogs. Napoleon and Lafayette had been snoozing by a haystack when they heard Edgar's motorbike approaching and decided to chase it.

"Charge!" shouted Napoleon.

In his surprise, Edgar lost control of the motorbike. The basket holding the sleeping kittens tumbled from the bike and landed under a bridge.

Edgar was long gone when the cats began to wake up.

"Uh-oh," said Toulouse. "It wasn't a dream. Edgar did this."

Meanwhile, back in Paris, Madame and Roquefort were beside themselves with grief. They couldn't find Duchess or the kittens anywhere.

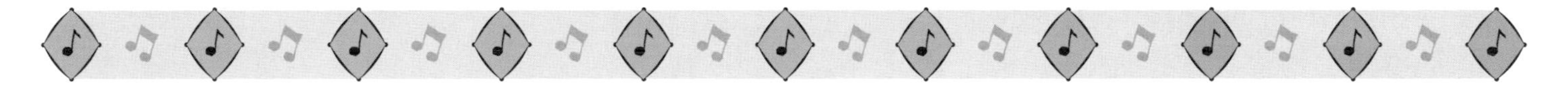

The next day, as Duchess pondered what to do, an orange alley cat happened by. The cat introduced himself as Abraham DeLacey Giuseppe Casey Thomas O'Malley. Duchess thought he was quite dashing.

O'Malley thought Duchess was beautiful. He offered to help her get back to Paris.

"We shall fly to Paris on a magic carpet, side by side, with the stars as our guide. Just we two . . . ," said O'Malley, just as the kittens emerged from hiding. " . . . three, four, five." O'Malley continued counting as the kittens made their presence known.

He hadn't realized that three kittens would be traveling with them. That would make the trip too difficult. But as he watched the family walk slowly away, he decided to help after all.

O'Malley spotted a truck headed for Paris. He helped Duchess and the kittens climb inside. They made it halfway to Paris when the driver discovered them and shooed them away.

The cats set out for Paris on foot. They came to a railroad bridge, but before they could get all the way across, a train came barrelling at them! O'Malley helped the cats to safety beneath the bridge. Marie lost her footing and tumbled into the river below. O'Malley dashed to the rescue. He jumped in after her, clung to a log, and was able to grab Marie. He passed her up to her mother and saved the day.

O'Malley finally managed to get Duchess and the kittens safely back into Paris. But Madame's mansion was on the other side of the city.

The kittens were bushed.

"I'll bet we walked a hundred miles," said Berlioz.

"I'll bet it's more than a thousand," replied Toulouse.

O'Malley led Duchess and the kittens to his home for the night. They were pleasantly surprised to find O'Malley's alley cat friends inside. The alley cats were splendid musicians. They sang, danced, and played instruments all night long. Duchess and the kittens happily joined in.

O'Malley explained to Duchess that these pals of his were the kind of friends everyone should have.

"They're a little rough around the edges," said O'Malley, "but if you're ever in a jam—*wham!* —they're right there."

The music and dancing came to an end and Duchess tucked the kittens in for the night. Duchess and O'Malley sat atop the roof and gazed at the moon. The two cats had fallen in love.

Duchess and O'Malley wished they could stay together. The kittens had grown very fond of O'Malley, too. They wanted him to become their father. But Duchess knew they had to return to their home. Madame must miss them very much.

O'Malley accompanied the family back to the mansion.

"Maybe just a short, sweet good-bye would be easiest," said O'Malley.

"I'll never forget you, Thomas O'Malley," said Duchess.

Duchess and the kittens went inside. Roquefort was excited to see them and tried to warn them about Edgar, but his warnings were in vain. The butler quickly scooped up the cats and put them in a sack.

"I told you it was Edgar," said Toulouse.

"Aw, shut up, Toulouse," said Berlioz.

Edgar took them to the barn and locked them in a crate headed for Timbuktu. Roquefort knew he had to act fast. He caught up with O'Malley and told him what had happened. After sending Roquefort to find his alley cat friends, O'Malley raced to the barn.

The battle was on. Roquefort showed up with the alley cats just in time. The little mouse worked diligently to get the lock open as the alley cats attacked Edgar. The lock popped open and O'Malley lifted the lid. He jumped in to help the kittens to safety, but Edgar broke free and slammed the lid shut. O'Malley, Duchess, and the kittens were trapped inside.

The alley cats attacked Edgar again. They dropped a bale of hay right on his head. Then they attached a hook to his suit jacket and swung him through the air. Edgar's feet hit the crate, knocking the lid open. O'Malley, Duchess, and the kittens leaped to safety. Then Frou Frou, Madame's horse, gave Edgar a fine horse kick. The greedy butler landed right inside the crate. The lid shut and the crate bounced out of the barn. As luck would have it, the delivery truck was just pulling up. Soon it was Edgar who was on his way to Timbuktu!

Duchess and the kittens returned to the mansion. Madame Adelaide was delighted they were home. She eagerly welcomed O'Malley into the family. After a family portrait, she revealed another surprise. Downstairs, they were greeted by their alley cat friends. The cats were playing their instruments, and everyone began dancing. Madame let all of the cats stay at her home, where they all lived happily ever after.

The Fox and the Hound

Story adapted by Gayla Amaral

From her perch high in a tree, a wise old owl named Big Mama watched hunting dogs furiously chase a fox. When the mother fox left her baby in a safe place, Big Mama knew she must find someone to care for it. And she knew the perfect person — Widow Tweed!

"Well, bless my soul!" exclaimed the widow upon discovering the fox cub hidden in her laundry. "It's a baby fox! I wonder where the mother is."

"You're such a little toddler," murmured the kind woman, as she fed the hungry cub a bottle of milk. "That's what I'll call you — Tod!"

Meanwhile down the road, Amos Slade's rickety old truck sputtered up to his house. His old dog, Chief, sniffed suspiciously as the hunter held out something squirming in a sack.

"How's this for a huntin' dog?" the old hunter asked as he opened the sack to reveal a whimpering little puppy. "His name is Copper."

Being older, Chief didn't want to play like Copper did, but he had to admit, the puppy was cute.

Tod was having the time of his life in his new home—and causing quite a stir in the barn and the henhouse. Widow Tweed shooed him out of the barn, gently warning him, "And try to stay out of mischief."

Soon Tod found something new to play with—a butterfly! He followed the butterfly through the woods. It led him straight to an old log.

Tod was unaware that Copper was sniffing his way toward the same log. *Sniff! Sniff!* Copper smelled something he had never smelled before. He just had to follow the scent, and he wandered down the trail away from his home.

"Whatcha smellin'?" asked Tod, poking his furry head inside the log to watch the curious pup.

"I'm on the trail of somethin'," replied Copper. He followed his nose around the log some more until he finally came face to face with Tod. "Why, it's you!" he added, thrilled to have tracked down the scent.

Copper immediately began howling, but it was just a little puppy howl. Tod wasn't scared a bit.

"I'm a fox. My name is Tod," said the friendly little cub. "What's your name, kid?"

"My name is Copper, and I'm a hound dog," answered the pup.

"Gee, I bet you're good at playing hide-and-seek," said Tod as they played. It was the beginning of a beautiful friendship.

"Copper, you are my best friend," said Tod with a smile. "We'll be friends forever, won't we?"

Copper agreed, "Yeah, forever."

Amos called Copper home and tied him to his doghouse. Later, when Tod came to visit his buddy, Chief suddenly woke up and began chasing Tod! *Bam! Bam!* It was Amos with his shotgun. Thankfully, he missed.

Poor Tod! Now he had to stay cooped up in the house. One day, Tod watched Amos pack his truck to take his dogs on a long hunting trip. Tod watched sadly as Copper rode out of sight.

Big Mama warned Tod that Copper would be trained to hunt and that it would change their friendship. But Tod refused to believe it.

Autumn and winter came and went. Spring arrived, and Copper was now a prized hunting dog. He returned home, reuniting the fox and the hound. Although they were glad to see one another, Copper warned Tod, "You're going to get us both in trouble."

"We're still friends, aren't we?" asked a confused Tod.

"Those days are over. I'm a hunting dog now," replied Copper. Tod did not understand why things had to be different.

Suddenly, Chief awoke! Barking and snarling at Tod, Chief began to chase him. Amos came running out of the house, chasing Tod as well. Copper, following his new hunting instincts, joined the hunter and Chief as they chased Tod into the forest. As Chief pursued Tod down the railroad tracks, the old hunter gleefully exclaimed, "Ol' Chief's got him on the run!" Without warning, a train steamed around the bend, forcing Chief off the tracks and into the river below.

Chief was hurt. Copper stood over him and was furious at Tod. Copper felt that Tod was responsible for hurting Chief.

"I'll get you for this, Tod, if it's the last thing I do!" growled Copper, as he looked sadly at the injured Chief.

Tod could hardly believe his ears and quickly ran home to safety. Widow Tweed knew what had to be done. Tearfully, she hugged Tod good-bye and took him to the game preserve where he would be safe from hunters like Amos Slade.

Tod felt alone in the world. Then he met Vixey, the most beautiful lady fox he had ever seen! What fun they had running and playing together!

But the fun soon ended. Even in the game preserve, Tod wasn't safe from Amos and his old friend, Copper. Growling and yelping, Tod and Copper circled one another. Baring his teeth, Copper was determined to get Tod and avenge his friend, Chief. But just when it appeared they had captured Tod, he miraculously escaped their trap!

Growl! Suddenly, they looked up, and looming above Amos was a huge, black bear! Copper fought courageously to save his master, but the hound was soon in danger himself.

But loyal friendships don't die easily, and Tod was not about to let the bear hurt his old friend. He led the bear away from Amos and Copper. No sooner had Tod helped them both escape the bear when he found himself looking down the barrel of Amos Slade's gun! But what was Copper doing?

"Come on, Copper! Get out of the way!" the hunter shouted. But Copper didn't move. He stood protectively over Tod, pleading with Amos to let his old friend live.

As the old hunter looked at the two friends, he smiled. Realizing the depth of the friendship between the fox and the hound, he sighed, "Well, let's go home, Copper."

Back at home Copper and Chief took their usual spots outside the house. Looking over at Chief snoring beside him, Copper smiled and settled down for a nice, long nap, too. As he drifted off, he couldn't help but hear a voice from the past.

"Gee, I bet you're good at playing hide-and-seek," Tod had said on the day the two unlikely friends had met one year ago. They had been through a true test of their friendship, and they passed with flying colors.

Copper remembered a conversation they had had long ago.

"Copper, you are my very best friend," said Tod. "And we'll be friends forever, won't we?"

"Yeah, forever," agreed Copper.

Story adapted by Lora Kalkman

Near the edge of the Great Barrier Reef in Australia, a clownfish named Nemo lived with his father, Marlin. Because Nemo was his only child, Marlin was very protective of him. One of Nemo's fins was smaller than the other, so Marlin always worried about Nemo's ability to swim.

On Nemo's first day of school, Nemo and his classmates excitedly jumped on the back of their teacher, Mr. Ray. Mr. Ray was taking them on a trip to the Drop-off, which was at the edge of the reef, near the deep part of the ocean. When Marlin learned of the plan, he worriedly swam after them.

When he arrived at the Drop-off, he saw Nemo's friends daring each other to swim out past the edge toward a boat anchored overhead. Marlin scolded Nemo, even though he had done nothing wrong. Marlin reminded Nemo that he couldn't swim very well. Nemo didn't like hearing that.

While Marlin was busy talking with Nemo's teacher, Nemo, eager to demonstrate that he could swim as well as anyone despite his small fin, swam to the boat to prove his father wrong.

Much to Nemo's horror, a scuba diver swam up and captured him! Nemo was taken aboard the boat while the others watched helplessly. Marlin tried to swim after the boat, but it quickly sped away.

Marlin was frantic. "Has anyone seen a boat?" he asked all the fish swimming nearby. "They took my son!"

A regal blue tang fish named Dory offered to help.

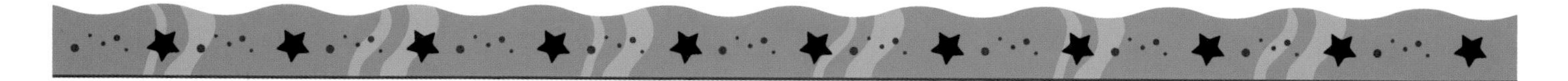

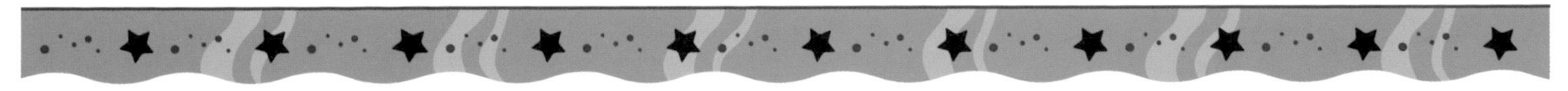

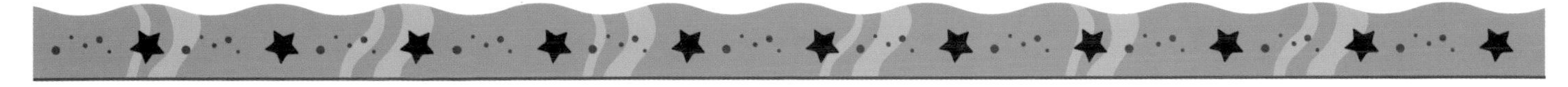

"I saw a boat," she said. "Follow me!" But Dory later admitted that she had a terrible memory. She couldn't remember anything for very long. In fact, she had even forgotten why Marlin was following her.

Suddenly, a giant shark named Bruce appeared. Bruce took the two fish to a sunken submarine for a meeting with other sharks. The sharks, in their desire to improve their image, were determined not to eat fish anymore. They wanted to prove they could all get along and be friends.

At the meeting, Marlin spotted a diver's mask. He realized it belonged to the diver who had captured Nemo. The mask had writing on it, but Marlin could not read it.

As Dory grabbed the mask, it snapped and hit her in the nose. A drop of her blood floated right into Bruce's nose. The smell of Dory's blood sent Bruce into a frenzy. He could not control himself. He wanted fish for dinner!

He chased after Marlin and Dory, hungrily snapping his jaws. The other sharks tried to stop him, without success. Marlin and Dory had to think fast. They raced into the submarine's torpedo launcher. Dory launched a torpedo right into Bruce's mouth. Bruce angrily spit the torpedo out of his mouth without realizing that it was headed for an underwater floating mine! The torpedo hit the mine and exploded.

Luckily, when the dust settled from the blast, Marlin and Dory still had the mask—the only clue to finding Nemo.

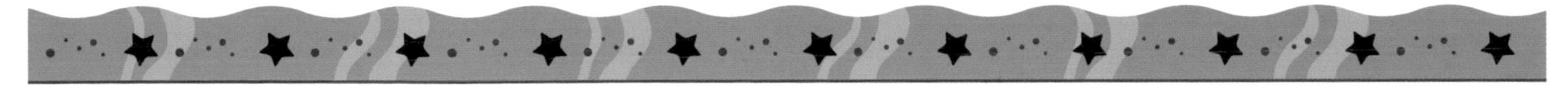

Kerplunk! A frightened Nemo was dropped into a fish tank. The scuba diver, a dentist named Dr. Sherman, had taken Nemo to his office.

Nigel, a pelican, swooped by to say hello to all of his fish friends in the tank. When the dentist shooed the bird away, he accidentally knocked over a photo of a little girl named Darla. Nemo soon learned that Darla was Dr. Sherman's niece and he, Nemo, was going to be her birthday present. To make matters worse, Darla did not know how to care for fish.

Just then, a fish named Gill swam over to introduce himself. Gill was the leader of the tank. Like Nemo, he, too, had a damaged fin. The two fish became fast friends. Gill eagerly explained that he had an escape plan.

Meanwhile, Dory and Marlin had to devise their own escape plan. Dory had dropped the diver's mask into a deep trench. Swimming down to retrieve it, the two fish encountered a fierce anglerfish with a glowing antenna. Marlin tried to keep the light nearby without getting eaten, while Dory read the writing on the mask.

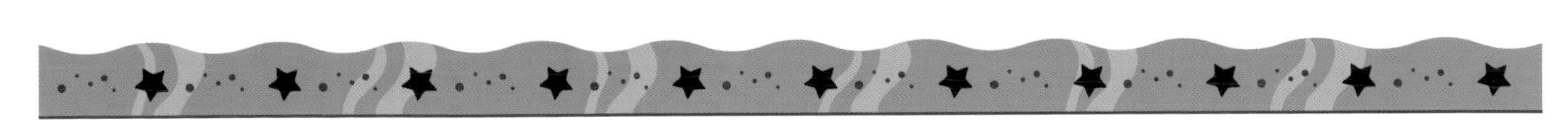

Marlin and Dory had the address of the scuba diver—42 Wallaby Way, Sydney. Now they had to figure out how to get there. They stopped to ask a school of moonfish for directions to Sydney. The moonfish gave directions to Dory along with some advice. "When you come to a trench, swim through it, not over it," the moonfish warned her. But by the time they reached the trench, Dory had forgotten!

Unfortunately, Marlin tricked Dory into swimming over the trench. They were soon surrounded by hundreds of dangerous pink jellyfish! The jellyfish had poisonous tentacles that stung. Marlin, nervously watching Dory bounce on a jellyfish top, suggested they play a game.

"Whoever can hop the fastest on the tops of these jellyfish wins," he said. This way, the tentacles could not sting them. They had almost escaped when Dory was stung! Marlin bravely pulled her out of the jellyfish forest, but he was also stung. Weak and tired, the two fish passed out.

Back in the tank, Gill was preparing Nemo for the great escape. He explained how he'd tried to escape once before by jumping into the toilet. "All drains lead to the ocean, kid," he told Nemo.

Now Gill had another plan. They would break the filter in the fish tank. With the filter broken, the tank was likey to get dirty. While it was being cleaned, the fish would be placed in plastic bags. Then they could bounce out the window and into the harbor!

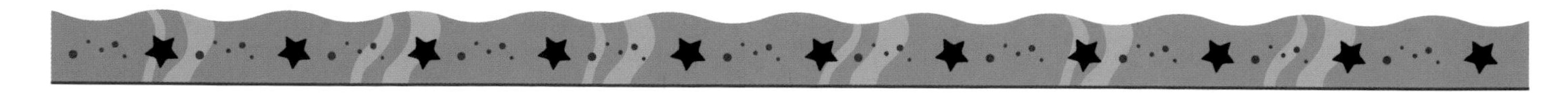

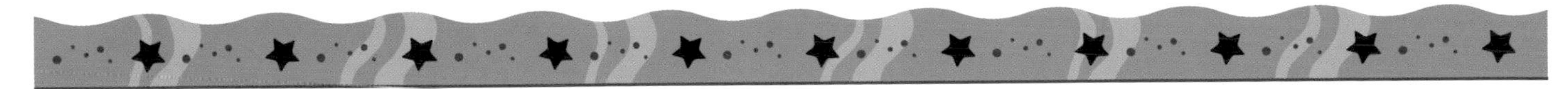

Nemo's job was to swim into the filter and wedge a pebble in the fan. The fish cheered when Nemo succeeded. The fan stopped! But as Nemo made his way back, the pebble came loose! The plan failed. How would Nemo escape now?

Meanwhile, a group of sea turtles rescued the weary Marlin and Dory. Crush, a surfer turtle, befriended them. He offered to let the fish ride with him on a current to Sydney. Marlin and Dory gladly accepted.

Marlin told the other turtles about his quest to find his son. The turtles, in turn, told other sea creatures. Soon, Marlin's story had spread throughout the vast ocean. Nigel the pelican overheard the news. He quickly flew to the dentist's office to tell Nemo.

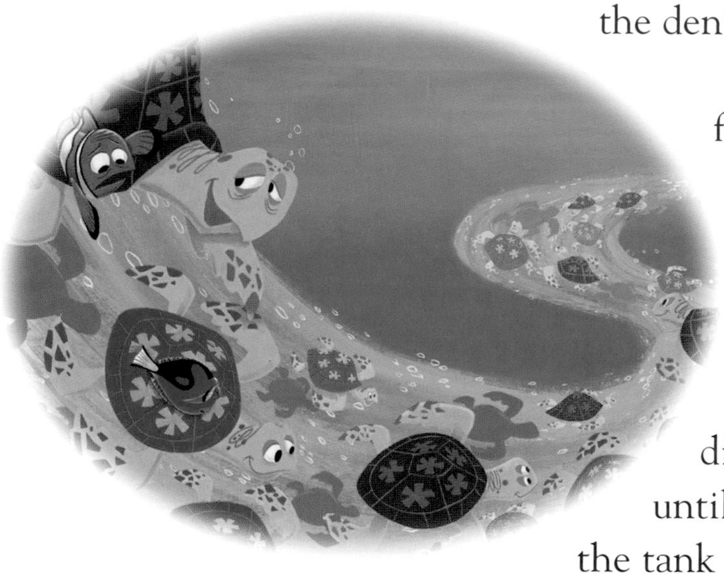

Nemo was inspired by his father's courage. He raced back into the filter. This time, Nemo succeeded in jamming a pebble squarely in the fan! Sure enough, with the filter not working, the tank started to get dirty. There were two days left until Darla arrived, so the fish hoped the tank would soon require cleaning!

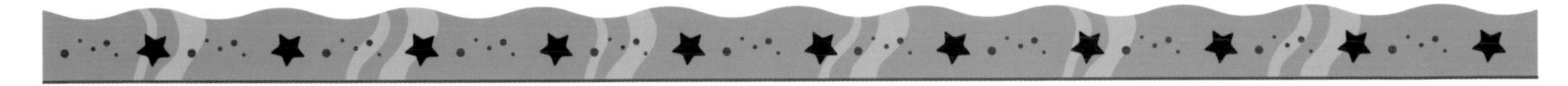

Crush and the sea turtles bid farewell to Marlin and Dory. The two fish had almost reached Sydney! They swam and swam, but soon realized they were lost. When a giant blue whale approached, Dory asked for directions. Unexpectedly, the little fish were sucked into the whale's gigantic mouth!

Back at the dentist's office, Dr. Sherman noticed his fish tank was slimy and green. "I'd better clean the tank before Darla gets here," he said. The escape plan was working! But by the next morning, the tank was perfectly clean. Dr. Sherman had purchased a new, high-tech filter called the Aqua Scum 2003. Now he would never have to clean the tank again. Sadly, the fish realized their escape plan had failed.

Swoosh! Outside Sydney Harbor, a blue whale surfaced and spouted. Dory and Marlin rode atop the spray. Marlin was excited to see many boats. He and Dory searched all night for the boat that took Nemo. Then a pelican swooped by and scooped them up.

Marlin was determined not to be eaten and lodged himself in the bird's throat. As the pelican choked on the two fish, Nigel came by and stopped to help his friend. He whacked the bird on the back, and the two fish landed on the dock. "I've got to find my son, Nemo," Marlin exclaimed. Nigel realized that this fish was Nemo's father.

Nigel snatched the two fish before a flock of hungry seagulls could get to them. They headed toward Dr. Sherman's office to rescue Nemo.

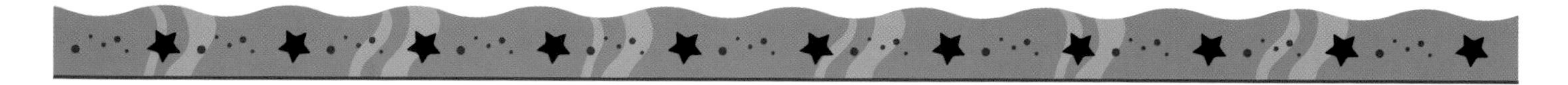

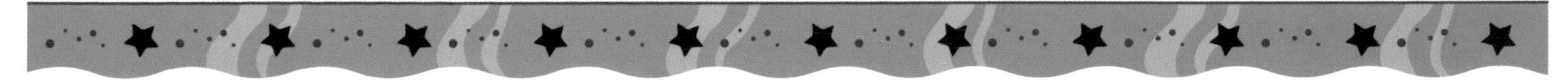

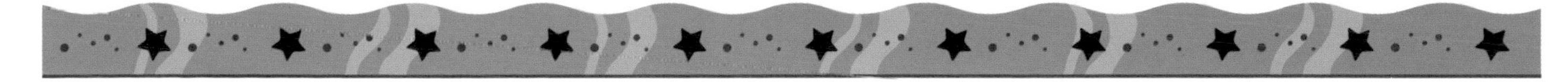

Back in Dr. Sherman's office, the dentist scooped Nemo from the tank and put him in a clear plastic bag. Darla was on her way. Nemo had an idea.

When Darla walked in, Nemo played dead. He hoped he would be flushed down the drain. Instead, Dr. Sherman headed for the trash can! Meanwhile, Nigel flew in through the window and startled Dr. Sherman, who dropped the bag. In a heroic effort to save his pal, Gill leaped out of the tank and launched Nemo into the spit sink. Nemo escaped down the drain!

Nigel dropped Marlin and Dory back into the sea. Marlin had seen Nemo floating in the bag and thought he was gone. Wanting to be alone, he left Dory. But Nemo, who was now safely back in the ocean, ran into Dory. Dory was delighted at being able to reunite Nemo and his father.

A few weeks later, Marlin and Nemo raced to the schoolyard. Marlin proudly watched his son go off on an adventure with his class. Suddenly, Nemo turned back to give his dad a hug.

"Love ya, Dad," said Nemo.

"I love you, too, son," said Marlin.